JAMES E. CHANDLER, JR.

ARE YOU KIDDING ME?

ONE SUNDAY NIGHT IN THE LIFE
OF DEACON WILLIE A.P. LESTER, JR.

WILLIE'S WORLD: BOOK I

SHOWITT ENTERTAINMENT
DOUGLASVILLE, GA

ARE YOU KIDDING ME?

This book is a work of fiction. Names, characters, places, and incidents are the product of the author's imagination or are used fictitiously. Any resemblance to actual events, locales, or persons, living or dead, is coincidental.

ARE YOU KIDDING ME? Copyright © 2015 by James Chandler, Sr.

ISBN 13: 978-0-692-37149-7

Published by Showitt Entertainment, Inc.
Douglasville, GA

Printed in the United States of America
First Edition February, 2015

Cover Design by Make Your Mark Publishing Solutions
Interior Layout by A Reader's Perspective
Editing by Make Your Mark Publishing Solutions

ARE YOU KIDDING ME?

ONE SUNDAY NIGHT IN THE LIFE
OF DEACON WILLIE A.P. LESTER, JR.

WILLIE'S WORLD: BOOK I

Acknowledgements

I would like to thank my gracious heavenly Father, who anointed me to begin and complete this work. I would not be able to begin this series without You guiding my hand and stretching my mind. All praise, glory, and honor belong to You, and I lift up Your name. In the beginning, this book was birthed as a stage play performed at my church, Marvelous Light Christian Ministries. The cast was comprised of members of the church and it's because of their tireless labor of love and hard work that this work was first seen by many on stage before being transformed into print.

A special thank you goes to Kelly Chandler, my wife and best friend, who believed from the very beginning and never doubted I could accomplish this God-given assignment. I love you for being the most incredible woman I've ever known in my life and you are a virtuous woman in every way. Thank you for reading every chapter I've written without complaining. Thank you for fixing and drinking coffee with me at all hours of the night as this book and the plays were being deposited into my spirit. Thank you for holding me up and lifting me up before the Lord. You've been my rock for nearly thirty-five years, and

I am who I am today because of you. Get ready, my love, the best is yet to come for both of us.

Kayla, J.C., and Jonathan, my children, who have always given me unconditional and unceasing love and constant support, know that you are the reason why I push as hard as I do to make a difference. You inspire me more than you know and I'm humbled and honored to have been blessed with such gifted, intelligent, spirit-filled, and amazing children. You are my inspirations, and I love you and thank you for all you've done for me and your mom. I would not dare forget to acknowledge and thank my precious grand baby, Lauryn. You're always so concerned about PaPa and you always want to let me know that everything's going to be all right. Your smile and heart are just the motivation I need to be better every day.

What can I say about my sister in Christ and business partner Cindy? You are a constant source of energy and strength, who always comes up with great ideas to expand the reach of my ministry. Your prayers pushed me to never give up. Thank you for being a true friend to my girl and praying for her and me daily.

Thank you Dad, Mom, David, Loretta, and Cloretta, my family, who honor me by allowing me to serve as your pastor. Our parents taught us as children to work together in ministry for the glory of God, but I never imagined that I would stand as your pastor in this season of our lives. I'm humbled by your love and always blessed by your gifts to the kingdom.

I would be remiss if I didn't give thanks to those incredible members who trusted their pastor's vision by performing in the play several years ago. I truly thank you, Kelly, Kayla, Dwain, Princilla, Tonya, Porsha, Mysia, Louise, Stephanie, Dana, Calai, Thor, Sherese, Tajuana, Marcus, Brian, Stanphanie, Phalonda, and Frost. I also must thank God for the best church family in the whole world: Marvelous Light Christian Ministries, I love each of you with all my heart and I appreciate your support and prayers.

Finally, to a special young lady who I've yet to meet in person, but I've already discovered how much of a blessing she is to me and this book: Thank you, Monique Mensah of Make Your Mark Publishing Solutions. From the first day we spoke on the phone I knew that God had directed me to the right person to edit and publish this work. You were very patient with me, and I appreciate your honesty and integrity.

To all of the readers who can identify with knowing one of these characters or who have laughed at the funny things that happen sometimes in church, I hope once you've read this book you'll continue to laugh and eagerly await the sequel. Remember, if you look hard enough, you'll see God moving in every situation.

INTRODUCTION

MY OFFICIAL NAME AND TITLE IS DEACON WILLIE A.P. LESTER, JR. Yes, that's right; I'm chairman of the deacon board down at the Auburn Avenue Missionary Baptist Church. Now, I've been a member of this church for over thirty years, and everybody who knows me knows that I speak my mind all the time. I really don't care who has a problem with what some call my straightforward and abrasive disposition. I am who I am. Now, I'm gonna be in the church house every Sunday morning, but because this pastor we got over here can't hardly preach, I gets gone right after the benediction and quickly find something to drink to calm my nerves.

The pastor is Dr. Charles David Weldon, III. Now, he's educated; I'll give him that. But I don't know if I agree with some of these folk that say he's a powerful, gifted, preaching machine, who has done enormous work in the community. I wouldn't go that far. You see, his first marriage ended in divorce after fourteen years, and you would think he would have made time to start a family, but he hasn't. He could have done some real good for this church and community, but in the last few years he's just lost focus on what's really important in life and ministry. I heard he's been having nightmares because of some stupid choices he'd recently made. You can't be playing with God and think He's not gonna get you.

I want to talk to you about some things that went down today after church. I'd left just before it got foolish in there. But my people have already told me about the madness. It's pretty late right now, but some hours ago, many of the members gathered for a meeting. I heard they'd gone to discuss what had happened in church this morning that ended with Pastor Weldon being arrested. Yep, they locked him up and hauled his butt right off to jail. How do I know it, you ask? Well, 'cause he was sitting right there in the cell next to mine. How did I get there? Don't worry about that right now; we're talking about Weldon.

Hold on, I'm getting ahead of myself. Let's start with what went down at the meeting tonight. Friendships were challenged and divisions started mounting all over the place. I normally don't even bother with other folk problems, but sometimes you just can't avoid getting dusty from all the dirt in the room. What began as a normal Sunday morning became something ridiculous. All I can say to what I've just heard is "Are you kiddin' me?"

CHAPTER 1: The Meeting

"Behold how good and pleasant it is for brethren to dwell together in unity" (Psalms 133:1).

NORMALLY, THE LAST PLACE YOU'D FIND THIS GROUP OF TRADITIONAL southern black Baptist parishioners on a late summer Sunday evening would be inside the church house for an emergency meeting. You see they lived by the rule that a good, upstanding Baptist need only attend the eleven a.m. worship service, and anything beyond that was an unnecessary ruse aimed at getting more money out of your pockets.

The prevailing thought was if you served on at least one auxiliary, paid your dues, wore black and white on First Sunday, and shook the deacon's hand during the right hand of fellowship, you were good. The benediction was recited religiously at 1:15 p.m. and after that, it was a race for the exit and the conclusion of another weekly ritual. So for cars to have turned into the parking lot for a church meeting was not only out of the norm, it was downright bizarre.

They tell me that Linda arranged this meeting, and by the pensive look on her face, it was quite evident she was not there to play games. Tonight's issues were intense, and she was very adamant that nobody was leaving until they found a complete and final resolution.

"Everyone, let's quiet down now and listen," she said sternly. "I'm ready to call this meeting to order, and I need your full and undivided attention."

I've known Linda ever since she was a little girl. Evangelist

Bell—that's what the church folk call her—is a no-nonsense southern bell, who grew up fast and hard in a racist upper scale suburb of North Atlanta. It seemed as if she always had to defend herself against spoiled little rich white girls, who thought their prestige and pedigree granted them special favor. Her father owned and operated three hardware stores on the south side of town but was insistent that his family would not be living in the area where he made his money. He always dreamed that his children would have the life he never knew and attend the schools where a pristine education was guaranteed by the generous donations of loyal alumni. It didn't matter that they were devoted, left-leaning, liberal democrats in a sea of Ronald Reagan republicans, or that they were the only black people in the immediate area, or even that they knew most of the neighbors didn't want this "darky" family living in the neighborhood. No, his only concern was that he expose his children to the finer things in life.

Linda would often listen to her father talk about the struggles of growing up poor and black in the Jim Crow South. He never got used to drinking warm water from Negro-only faucets and being forced to ride in the back of the bus or stand if a white person wanted his seat. He was adamant in teaching his children that they were as good as anyone else and not to allow anyone to speak to them disrespectfully. Linda grew up committed to the principle of standing your ground and exerting your will, and today she was doing just that.

"Hey, I said be quiet please," Linda continued. "I need each of you to take your seats right now so we can get this meeting started."

This went on for nearly ten minutes as she stood there trying to silence the murmurs and complaints that festered and grew louder each time the entry doors opened. The mass email message had clearly stated that tonight's meeting would begin promptly at seven p.m. But no matter what, you could always count on these church folk to show up when they felt like it, as if they needed others to notice their arrival. Even on Sunday mornings, some of these same aristocrats notoriously walked their trifling behinds into the sanctuary, right in the middle of the sermon. It wouldn't be so bad if they'd quietly come in and quickly find a seat in the back, but these clowns moved straight down the center aisle, waving their hands in the air, trying to get an usher to find them an opening down front.

"Say, preacher lady," Sharon interrupted, "now just how long this thang gonna last? I got stuff to do, and you already know I ain't tryin' to be here all night with y'all Negroes!"

Sharon is one of those bright yellow self-proclaimed divas, who swears that the sun rises and sets on her big, voluptuous tail. She is certain that every man wants to sleep with her and every woman is jealous of her. She reasons that because, at forty-three, she still has the legs of a nineteen-year-old gymnast and a figure like Beyoncé, everybody is trying to get with her. Now she does have some wonderfully sculptured, round, perky breasts that protrude valiantly through every tight-fitting sweater she wears, oh yes, Lord! What I like is that she isn't the least bit ashamed to bring attention to them, and I'm not the least bit ashamed to notice them. Anyway, these rookie husbands in church are always getting in trouble with their wives for staring just a little longer than they should. There is no denying the fact that she is a strikingly beautiful woman, but unfortunately an aroma of arrogance oozes from her pores, making it difficult for women to like her and spend much time in her company.

Sharon told me one day that she was brought up on the south side of Chicago in a very poor, crime-ridden and diverse neighborhood. Her father was an African American steel worker and truck driver, and her mother was a beautiful, undocumented Puerto Rican woman, who cleaned houses and stayed under the radar. Just like Linda, Sharon had to fight all the time growing up. The black kids said that she thought she was better than them because she had long hair, hazel eyes, and light skin. The Hispanic children in the community shunned her because, to them, she tried to act too black, especially at block parties and school events. Sharon ran away to Atlanta at sixteen and ended up living in a group home on the west side of town. She was determined not to end up like her mother and father; so somehow, someway she enrolled into Harper High School and graduated a year ahead of time.

"Excuse me?" Linda sarcastically replied to Sharon. "Let me remind you that *you* don't run this meeting, and you sure don't run me! Just find a seat, and I'll let you know when it's time to leave."

Sharon and Linda have been a part of this church for many years, and though they respect one another's gifts and abilities, they have little regard and time for each other. Linda, after graduating high school, went on to attend Oral Roberts University, where she received her bachelor's degree in Religion and Philosophy and her master's in Clinical Psychology. Sharon attended Spelman College and finished near the top of her class with a degree in Business Finance. Linda currently serves as an associate minister under Pastor Weldon and Sharon is a church trustee and the president of the gospel choir. They are extremely effective in their specified areas of concentration, but getting them to work together as a team is as likely as getting the grand wizard of the Ku Klux Klan to endorse Michelle Obama as the next president of the United States.

"Oh, wait a minute," Sharon snapped back. "Don't get sassy with me, heifer! I don't care whose meeting this is. Just understand that my time is not to be wasted, so whatever you brought us out here to discuss, you need to get to it now, 'cause I've got things to do."

These two are always fussing about something and if the conflict isn't verbal, it can easily be seen in their overt expressions of dislike and distrust. Sharon feels that Linda looks down on everyone who hasn't graduated from a snooty Ivy League school, and Linda's impression of Sharon is that she is nothing more than a street hustler, masquerading as a devoted church member. Each is wrong about the other, but you can't get them to see anything different than what they believe. It's like trying to mix hot grease with cold water, and it doesn't take much provocation at all for one of them to jump off at the mouth, and then it's on and poppin' for real.

One of the female guards at the jail is also a member of the church and she was at the meeting tonight. She told me that the two ladies continued slinging smart comments at one another, and the more they locked horns, the closer they drew toward each other. Sharon's fists were clinching with each forward step and she was just about to haul off and slap fire out of Linda's mouth, until Mary jumped between them.

"Oh, I know you fools are not up in my God's house clowning like a couple of backed up, snaggletooth, starved and diseased, homeless alley cats! Y'all up in here acting like you ain't got no home training—no home training a'tall!"

Sister Mary Ethel-Maye Stevens—that's my girl. She's a ballsy, no-nonsense woman, who was once a tremendously sought after evangelist in her day. A series of traumatic events had stolen three decades of her life, and this one-time prolific and poetic pulpiteer is now an overweight, homeless street preacher. Mary spent nearly thirty years of her life pillaging on the streets and back alleys of the big city, doing whatever it took to survive. She just recently reconnected with the church she once loved and served so well. When her family finally found her, she was out by a dumpster wearing an assortment of discarded clothes and eating food out of a greasy brown paper bag. Mary battles with schizophrenia and depression but was determined to get her life back. She had enough sense to know that the best place for her to make that change is in the house of the Lord. She had no idea, however, that when she came to church this morning she would end up being a participant in a scandalous church meeting that same evening.

"Y'all acting like your mamas ain't never took yo' tail nowhere or taught you how to act in someone else's house," Mary continued. "You up in here with your nasty shoes on when Granny told you five times to scrape that mud off yo' feet outside!"

Linda is Mary's baby sister, but even she had never seen her going off like this, not even while bouncing in and out of reality.

"One of y'all done let the next-door neighbor's bad little children up in here," Mary went on. "Dem nappy-headed heathens done got crayon scribblings all over the wall!"

By this time, the room had gone completely silent as everyone stood there stunned and stupefied, wondering if this plus-sized, loud-talking woman was slipping into the twilight zone. People slowly backed away from her because they knew that no matter what she was bellowing, it was best to give her plenty of room to have this discussion alone.

She rolled up the sleeves on her dress, hiked up her knee-high pantyhose, grabbed a cardboard fan out of the top of her bosom, kicked off her shoes, and stood up on a chair in the middle of the room. "And you over there," she said while pointing to a young man who had just walked into the room, chewing on a Snickers candy bar, clearly unprepared for this unprovoked onslaught. "You ain't took out the trash or loaded the dishwasher in two days, so now we can't eat no collard greens and cornbread 'cause all the dishes are dirty!" All of a sudden she started screaming at the top of her lungs, digging and scratching into the wig atop her head and jumping up and down in the chair, yelling, "Lord Jesus, just look at all these little cockroaches and water bugs running around here, lookin' for cookies that y'all done let fall behind the sofa! These vermin carry diseases, and I don't have enough medicine but for only three of y'all."

The room that had been bone silent sixty seconds before erupted as one person after the other jumped, screamed, and swatted imaginary insects and rodents. Two men climbed up on a table, clutching each other and hollering like little girls. Three of the choir members cleared out the first four rows of chairs, trying to get to the exit. It was a hot mess in there.

"Lady," Sharon yelled, "get your big tail out of that chair and stop acting a darn fool in here! What in the hell are you talking about?"

Mary immediately stopped moving, slowly turned around, and stepped down from the chair. She looked piercingly into Sharon's eyes like she was about to open up a can of whoop ass.

"What am I talking about?" Mary replied. "I'm talking about the fact that since y'all in here driving my sister crazy because you won't sit down and listen, the best thing to do is talk crazy to folk who are *crazy*! Now sit yo' little pompous, no-singing, three-dollar-weave-wearing, snaggletooth self down and shut up so we can get to this meeting!"

"I know you heard that!" Q.T. chimed in, laughing loudly. "That old lady said sit your non-singing, big-lipped, pigeon-toed, bucktooth self down and quit runnin' off at the mouth all the time!"

I don't know how in the world we ended up hiring this minister of music by the name of Quincy LaVelle Thomaston. Everybody calls him Q.T., and to say that he is flamboyant and pretentious is a grand understatement, if I ever say so myself. I ain't never cared for the boy because he walks around church shaking and shifting more than the single women looking to catch a man. He'll make your stomach tighten up in knots watching him direct the choir. God knows I've tried my best to ignore him and even forget I ever met him, but that's impossible because he's nauseously unforgettable. I understand that he and my little precious friend Portia had words at the meeting. Shoot, who didn't have words?

"Q.T.," Portia said, "you need to get your attitude in check! I heard you this afternoon after church saying a lot of ugly things about Pastor Weldon to those sissy friends of yours, and I don't appreciate it!" She snapped her neck from left to right as she walked toward Q.T., reading him and squashing his attack on Sharon.

Portia is a smart, small-framed, courageous eighteen-year-old mother, who dearly loves and respects her Man of God. She tells everybody that Weldon stood by her side and shut down the gossipers when she became pregnant with little Amanda at fifteen. I knew her father pretty well, but he was in and out of jail most of her life. She's got an older brother, but this fool is always running around with a bunch of thugs in the neighborhood. People are always whispering and pointing at her when she enters the room with her baby girl, but she doesn't care about that. She's used to it. What she wasn't going to tolerate was somebody talking about someone she loved.

"You don't have the right to talk about anybody, Q.T.!" Portia yelled. "I didn't appreciate what you said earlier, and I don't appreciate how you're talking to Miss Sharon now!"

My source told me that there were a lot of folk in that meeting and everybody had something to say. You would think that they would just be quiet, at least until they got some clarity on what Weldon had done to get himself locked up, but nope, they didn't. Leona was there from the diner, along with her waitress Martha. Elaine and her daughter Portia were there because they love Weldon big time. Linda was trying her best to bring order to the meeting, but people were always getting their two cents in.

"Elaine," Leona said, "you better get your little fast-tail daughter and teach her how to respect adults and stay out of gown folk business! That's what's wrong with these young folk now; they don't know when to just be seen and not heard."

Elaine was about to go off on Leona for her unrequested statement about her daughter, but before she could say anything, Sharon jumped back in with both feet.

"Leona," Sharon said, "I know you're not sticking up for RuPaul over here."

"It's not about sticking up for Q.T.," Leona replied. "It's about teaching these kids some respect for their elders."

Leona ain't even fifty years old yet, but she has an old-school spirit. She owns Mama Mattie's Soul Food Restaurant, which was started by her mother and father over forty-five years ago. She had been working for her parents since she was a little girl, and when they passed away several years ago she vowed to keep the business going no matter what. Her parents were both in their mid-forties when she was born and she was the only child in a very religious and hard-working home. They'd raised her with strong, old-fashioned values. They'd taught her to always show respect to her elders.

Q.T. is no more than ten years Portia's senior, but it didn't matter to Leona. Right is right, and since he is older, that means that he is automatically due a certain amount of respect.

Leona turned her attention toward Sharon, who had helped herself into the discussion Leona was having with young Miss Portia. She was about to address what Sharon had said, but before she could open her mouth, Sharon picked up where she'd left off. "Leona, you're up in here defending Miss Thang, and it's apparent that you haven't seen his post about you on Facebook. Girl, he talked about how nasty the food tastes at your diner."

"Excuse me!" Leona yelped.

"Oh yeah. Since you don't know about that then you must also be in the dark about the way he told all of social media that your two-dollar-stripper waitress here received her education out of a Cracker Jack box. Child, he's got a copy of your dinner menu posted with pictures of what food is *supposed* to look like and what it looks like in your place."

"I don't have time to listen to this!" Leona proclaimed as she threw her hand up toward Sharon's face.

"Well, you better make time. He's got some kind of icon on the page and when you click on it, a copy of your menu pops up. The header, 'Smothered Pig Feet on Sale for $7.99' appears, but when it does, there's a picture of your big feet on the screen."

I told you that some of everybody was at this meeting, and

the guard told me that the longer it went on, the hotter it got. Word is that one of Weldon's old girlfriends brought her behind up in there tonight. The one I'm talking about is Kim. Kim is part owner and operator of Kutin' Up Beauty Salon and Barber Shop in the heart of downtown. She grew up in this area and has been doing hair since she was eleven years old. Now, I know she loves this church dearly, but sometimes the pressure she gets from a few of the long-time members makes her wonder just how much longer she can remain connected to this ministry.

It has been over fifteen years, and that's more than enough time to forget and forgive, but some people, even in the church, refuse to let go of your failures and just allow you to walk in the newness of life. You see, the rumor is that Kim and Pastor Weldon had a brief affair back then, and even though they've repented for the wrong they've done, there are those holier-than-thou members who look for any reason available to keep up mess and cause confusion.

"Sharon," Kim said, "you're probably the reason we're even having this meeting tonight in the first place. It seems like you're always starting something."

"Oh, I'm the reason?" Sharon shot back.

"Yeah! All you do is gossip and run your mouth about things you don't know anything about. You put rumors out there in the street about folk being with each other because you're all backed up and haven't had a man to take you out on a real date in years!"

"For real, Miss Kim?" Portia interrupted. "You talking about somebody and a man? You? For real?"

"Yes, I am," Kim said to Portia as she kept her focus on Sharon. "I'm sorry, Madam Choir President, but having your name monogramed on the back of a Happy Meal toy is not a gift a real man gives. You wouldn't know that, apparently, because that's what you're used to when all you can get is a piece o' man."

"Oh yeah? Well, you must have forgotten that I was out with your daddy last week!" Sharon snapped back with attitude.

I told y'all earlier that Leona and her waitress Martha were in the meeting, but I hadn't told you about Martha. Well, please let me tell you about this chick, here. Martha Antoinette Salano (that's how she introduced herself to me back when I met her) spent most of her formative childhood years on the streets of Spanish Harlem, going from shelter to shelter with a mother who was in and out of Upper Manhattan's drug treatment facilities. She learned self-defense by fending off her mom's numerous pimps and boyfriends, who regularly used her for a punching bag when the mood struck them. She never stayed more than a year in one school and eventually dropped out in the ninth grade after her mother got arrested for prostitution.

She grew up fast, which is evident by her tough demeanor, street smarts, and physical appearance. By the time she turned eleven, this child already had the body of a twenty-one-year-old woman, and men were relentlessly trying to introduce her to a lifestyle fit for someone well beyond her years. No fourteen-year-old girl should have spent her birthday getting an abortion, but this was the memory she was left with and the horror she endured. After years of hustling on the streets and picking up side gigs wherever she could, she decided to leave the Big Apple and try to discover what life is supposed to be like somewhere else. She stuffed what few clothes she had in a backpack, bought a one-way bus ticket, and headed to Atlanta, with nothing but hope and desire for a better life.

She told me that her bus pulled up to the station late in the afternoon and once she stepped off, there was nothing and no one to meet her but stiffness in her shoulders and an aching pain in her stomach. The trip was long and she was hungry. She'd spent the last dollar she had on that bus ticket, and now she found herself standing on the sidewalk in front of Mama Mattie's Diner, saying a little prayer that God would make a way somehow. Within only minutes of standing there, the front door opened and out walked Leona. She took one look at Martha and said, "It looks like you need a job and I need a waitress. Give me that bag. If you can get me through this dinner rush then you're hired." That was sixteen years ago.

Martha came to the meeting tonight just to support her boss, Leona, but when Mary had decided to insult her along with the others, she chose not to just sit there and take it. "Wait a minute, wait a minute, wait *just* one minute!" Martha suddenly yelled out. "Let's back this whole thing up! Everybody, move outta my way so I can get to this old lady over here! First of all," she said to Mary, "don't come in here calling me crazy, street lady! Now I did my time at Georgia Regional, and I don't care what y'all heard about me! Yeah ... I stabbed that fool, but it was in self-defense. I told that judge that black robes make me nervous. He could have worn something else, but he just had to wear that black one. So don't be calling me crazy. I hate that! I don't like it when people call me crazy!"

Normally, Martha was stable and very bright, but there were times when she would step back and forth between the two worlds of sanity and lunacy, and apparently this was one of those times.

"Oh my God!" Q.T. chimed back in. "I knew it! I told y'all but y'all wouldn't listen. I told y'all little Freddie Kruger's whacko mama escaped, but y'all acted like you couldn't hear me.

Y'all might want to leave this one alone, 'cause she looks like she's about to snap, and I'm not trying to be nobody's collateral damage up in here!"

"Whatever, Q.T.," Portia said. "You can't even spell collateral."

The funniest part about what happened at the meeting is when Elaine went off on Kim. See, Elaine Davis is one of those members who doesn't care for Kim at all. It doesn't matter how long it has been since the alleged affair ended; she feels that Kim should have removed herself from the church and gone on her way. Elaine is Portia's mother and one of the first new members to join the church under Pastor Weldon's leadership many years ago. She always talks about how he spoke life into her at a time when she was barely surviving a personal crisis. Whatever it was, it was crippling her health and destroying her family. She worked hard in the church, served in almost every ministry they had, and eventually became the pastor's personal administrative assistant. She takes pride in her position and became very protective of her shepherd. So when it became known that he and Kim had slept together, it hit her deeply.

Elaine is extremely intelligent and innovative and brings remarkable growth to the church from the structures and policies she has helped develop behind the scenes. Her loyalty is to Pastor, not Kim at all, so it not only seemed plausible, but dead-on right to blame Kim for seducing Weldon and tempting him into a tryst he would have otherwise not been a part of.

Linda saw Elaine's anger and knew that she was about to blow, so she tried to quickly defuse the freshly lit firecracker. "Elaine, don't!" Linda said. "This is not the time to deal with—"

"Oh no!" Elaine replied. "This *is* the time. Lady Weldon and I were the best of friends and she and Pastor were very happy together until this thang showed up in here looking like she just left the club."

"I'm not going to stand here and let you talk about me like that, Elaine!" Kim shouted.

"I don't care where you stand, but you're going to hear this. I watched you weasel yourself into their lives, claiming that God sent you to be First Lady's armor bearer, when all along you just wanted to get your filthy hands on her husband. Your little revelation in church this morning may have been news to most of these people, but I've known about you from the beginning, and it's women like you who bring good men down."

Oh yeah, I forgot to tell you about what happened this morning before church even got started. I understand that Kim and Saundra, her attorney friend that I'll tell you about later, were in the women's lavatory, talking about something or another. Well, when they walked in, there were other ladies already inside, doing whatever a bunch of ladies do at the same time in the bathroom. Anyway, during the conversation it got out that Kim had admitted that she and Weldon were in an affair years ago. She claimed that it ended way back when, but I'm not sure about that. Who cares? All I know is up until today, it was only a rumor, but after the revelation it's now confirmed.

Okay, let's get back to the meeting. The word is that slanderous, derogatory, and abusive comments were released from every corner of the room. The same worshippers, who just this morning were seen dancing and praising God, were now clowning and hollering all over the place. The teenagers started videoing and taking pictures on their cell phones like they were sitting down ringside at a cage fight. Fists were flying, wigs were thrown, shoes were coming off, and these saints clearly proved that they had not forgotten how to orchestrate a barrage of cuss words when needed. This meeting was out of control and was headed toward an all out Sunday-night brawl.

Just then Linda pulled a bullhorn from out of the file cabinet near the back door and yelled, "Q.T., Elaine, Martha, Sharon, Kim, Portia, Leona, Mary, Greg, Marsha, Peter, Jan, Bobby, Cindy, Alice ... dang it! Everybody, that's enough!"

For the second time tonight the room went bone silent, but this time not from shock, but fear. In all the years that Linda has been a member of this church, no one has ever heard her say anything close to a cuss word. She's been hurt, frustrated, disappointed, wounded, disturbed, flustered, irritated, aggravated, and even blatantly disrespected, but nothing ever, until now, has brought this tiny evangelist to a point of near profanity. The veins in her forehead were protruding, her shaking fists were clutched tightly, and her nerves were shot from all of the bickering.

"Now sit down and be quiet before you make my pressure go through the roof!" she screamed. "You already know I battle with these heart palpitations, and we are not going to bring this foolishness up into the Lord's house! There has been enough drama today, and it ends right now! I just thank my God that tight-dress-wearin', loud-talkin', chicken-eatin', hoochie-mama thing is not here tonight."

Before Linda could finish the sentence, the doors swung open and in walked Big Wanda. Describing Wanda as a little loud and somewhat talkative is like portraying Jaws to a group of fifth graders as a little fish that they could easily catch with a K-Mart knock-off fishing pole. She is one of the hair stylists at Kim's beauty shop, who regularly and happily provides all the patrons with the day's juiciest and most salacious gossip. If there's dirt on anyone, you can bet your last dollar that this one knows all about it. And it doesn't matter how much of it is true; if it needs some flavoring to spice it up, she'll just make up the rest.

Wanda speaks her mind and has an opinion on every topic under the sun, and she quickly offers that opinion to everybody, whether they want to hear it or not. Strangely enough, she also has this obsession about being the next big diva superstar. Every week she's somewhere auditioning for another reality TV spot or strutting her size twenty-four into a modeling agency, swearing she's the next Naomi Campbell. She signs up to sing on whatever musical competition show that's currently filming in the city. It wouldn't be so bad for her to follow her dreams if she could actually act, dance, or sing, but the problem is she doesn't have any real talent. However, you can't tell her that.

"Heeeeeyyyyy, everybody!" she said loudly. "Wanda's in the house! That's right, I said Wanda's in the house. Go get the offering baskets! Have the nurses bring me some hot green tea. Tell all the second-string wannabes to stop hatin'. And the ladies, grab yo' men, 'cause once they get a good look at all this chocolate chip, they'll be breaking their necks tryin' to get to this cookie!"

Lawd, I sho wish I could have been there to see that for myself. I couldn't believe that girl was in church this morning eating fried chicken that she'd stolen from Popeyes. Her two home girls were right there with her and they are just as ratchet as she is. The three of them were pulling biscuits out of their pocketbooks and spilling hot sauce on the floor. Now who does that? The jail guard told me they walked into tonight's meeting eating more chicken. I knew Mary was gonna go off when she saw Wanda walk through that door.

"Umph, umph, umph," Mary grunted. "I knew it. That girl's gonna find some chicken somewhere."

"Lawd Jesus," Leona chimed in. "The first thing you need to do is get that food up out of here! Don't you know you're not supposed to be eating in this part of the church? This ain't no restaurant, fool."

"Your diner ain't either, but we eat up in there," Wanda quickly snapped back.

"Wanda," Kim said, "what are you doing in here? This is a private meeting for the members of the church. How did you even know about this?"

"Well, Kim, since you ran out this morning chasing Raylon, you missed the part toward the end when I walked down to the alter and joined the church, honey. If you hadn't been so busy trying to see if your preacher man boyfriend was going to jail or not, you would have seen that. Isn't that right, Evangelist Bell?"

"Yeah, something like that," Linda replied, sighing and shaking her head.

"Who cares?" Elaine interrupted. "We're not here to talk about her. We are here to talk about Pastor and what we're going to do as a family to help him."

"What we're going to do as a family?" Sharon asked. "Elaine, what we *need* to do is get to the truth about what he did that got the police all up in here this morning. I mean, who is this girl they said he supposedly killed? What else has he done that we don't know anything about?"

"I don't care what you think he did," Elaine rebutted. "I don't care what people are saying and insinuating at all. I believe my pastor when he says he did not hurt that young girl. Sharon, now you know he has always been there for me and my kids, and we are *not* going to abandon him when he needs us the most. You shouldn't either!" Elaine stood in front of everyone, looking primarily at her long-time friend, who was now raising her blood pressure. Her voice amplified several octaves and her eyes began to water as she fought back tears of anger and disappointment.

Out of the blue, Martha decided to open her mouth again and ask questions that didn't concern her at all. "Kim," Martha blurted out, "where is your friend the attorney? Why isn't she here? I thought she was going to represent him; at least that's what I heard. I don't see her anywhere. She was in church this morning. She saw everything that happened, and look, she didn't even come back tonight to let us know he has legal representation. Maybe she already feels he's guilty."

Portia didn't like where this conversation was going. She was there this morning when Officer Raylon Jackson had come in and tried to handcuff Weldon. Weldon had run off like a true perpetrator and thought he was going to get away. But he didn't.

"Evangelist Bell," Portia said, with tears forming in her eyes, "please just tell me what we need to do. I know I'm the youngest one here, but when I got pregnant, most of you in this church treated me like trash. My pastor was the only one who had my back and stood up for me. He didn't condone what I did, but he didn't condemn me either. My mama is right: it doesn't matter what he's done ... we are not going to leave him alone now."

"Hey, Portia, listen," Q.T. said with a sneer, "you don't have to worry, 'cause let me tell you somethin' ... Pastor ran out of here so fast this morning, you woulda thought his draws were on fire! I swear he looked like that Jamaican boy in the Olympics. Honey, he hit that street, kicked off them Stacy Adams, threw off that robe, and was gone!"

Laughter broke out in the room, but not everyone was amused, especially Elaine. This was not a laughing matter, and anyone who thought otherwise should have stayed away from this meeting. She could feel the tension building in her shoulders and nothing in recent years had her more upset than what was happening right before her eyes. How could these people, who sat in front of this man weekly, celebrating in the power of his preaching, now turn their backs on him and find humor in the crisis he was facing?

"Oh, wait a minute," Wanda belted out, still laughing at Q.T. "So ain't none of y'all heard yet?"

Sick by Wanda's presence but needing to find out what she was talking about, Elaine responded, "Heard what? What are you talking about?"

"Oh, girl, he ran, sho' nuff, but he didn't get too far. My girl told me earlier that y'all's handsome preacher man—I mean *our* fine pastor—was picked up a few hours ago downtown. Kim, your little lawyer girlfriend is probably down there at the precinct with him right now."

Portia jumped up immediately, grabbing her purse, and said, "Well come on, everybody. If Pastor's in jail, we need to go get him out right now. We don't need to be meeting about what to do; we know what to do. Let's just go get him. Come on! What are you waiting on?"

"What kind of church is this?" Martha asked indignantly. "Your pastor can do anything, and it's just all right? He can break laws, sleep with other women, get involved with known criminals, and the first thing y'all want to do is just go bail him out with no questions asked?"

"Lady," Portia snapped back, "I don't know you, and right now I don't care to know you. What I do know is *my* pastor has been falsely accused of things I know he did not do."

Division once again broke out in the room. People were pointing fingers in each other's faces and it seemed like the mayhem that had quieted for a minute had revived itself again. The old saying is true: "You can take church folk out of the street, but you can't take the street out of church folk."

"Listen, everyone!" Linda yelled. "We can't just rush downtown demanding his release. We have to have a plan, and we need to know exactly what we're dealing with here. Now Portia and the rest of you, just calm down and please sit back down so we can figure out what to do."

"Well, Linda," Elaine quickly declared, "you can stay here with all these little simpleminded folk if you want to. Get your little paper and pen together, and you all work out a plan. I'm on my way to get *my* pastor out of that jail! He's not going to spend a single night in that God-awful place. No one should have to."

"Now I wouldn't go as far as to say *no one*," Q.T. blurted out while overtly looking in Martha's direction. "Some folk might need to be behind some bars right now, child."

Kim felt the need to speak up and not only address what had been disclosed about her and Pastor's past, but she also needed to get some of these self-appointed judges in check. "I know what I did with Charles many years ago was wrong," she said. "And Elaine, I know you've never liked me, but first of all, please know that I wasn't in that relationship alone."

"Kim, we don't want to hear anything about what you have to say right now," Elaine declared.

"Well whether you want to hear it or not, I'm going to speak my mind. Now, it sure is funny how you can quickly love and forgive him for what he's done, but you can't seem to forgive me for doing the very same thing. That's why I don't hardly fool with you church folk!"

"Girl, you don't have to keep defending yourself," Leona

proclaimed. "We all know you was a hussy. People make mistakes all the time. We need to stop rehashing old news and deal with what's in front of us right now."

"Well, y'all go on down there and tell my fine new pastor that I'll come by and see him later on," Wanda said. "He gonna need a little healing and deliverance service, and baby, I've got just the right words to ease his troubled mind."

"Girl," Mary jumped in, "if you don't leave that man alone, I'm gonna snatch so much hair out your head that your future grandchildren gonna be bald! Now move out the way so we can go down here and see about this pastor! Come on, y'all!"

Mary grabbed her purse, pulled out her keys, hiked up her drooping pantyhose again, and headed toward the door. Several members followed her, but most of them just tossed up the deuces and went home. If I were there, I would have shut that meeting down early. I would have just put forth a motion to vote this joker out. He truly gets on my nerves, and I'm sure he works a lot of other folk's nerves too. It didn't go down like that because yours truly was not at the meeting. No, I was meeting with a correctional officer around that time.

Chapter 2: How We Do It

"No man can serve two masters: for either he will hate the one, and love the other; or else he will hold to the one, and despise the other. Ye cannot serve God and mammon" (St. Matthew 6:24).

On the other side of town, while the members of Auburn Avenue were discussing and debating the events of the day, there was another meeting taking place at my upstairs neighbor, Tina's, apartment.

Tina Turner-Johnson lives better than most in the heart of our ghetto and has her hand on the pulse of our community. Not much gets past her, and since she's lived in this same housing development all her life, there's not much she hasn't seen or heard. She's learned how to make the most out of a little and prides herself in being book savvy and street smart. She may have dropped out of high school at seventeen after becoming pregnant, but having only a GED has not slowed her down one bit. Her motto is "Do what you do to get what you want. Live for the now and forget what was lost."

She's a thirty-nine-year-old woman, who's still angry with God for allowing the only man she'd ever loved to be killed in Desert Storm. He had just graduated from East High and enlisted into the Army when she'd learned the summer of her junior year that she was pregnant with Kalitha. The two had talked about getting married once he completed boot camp and found out where he was going to be stationed, but to their surprise he was immediately deployed overseas and she never saw him or heard his voice again. Abandoned by her father, abused by her drugged-out mother, and crushed by the sudden loss of her man, the only thing that kept her going was this bowlegged princess, Kalitha.

Kalitha lives upstairs with her mother. I watched her raise this girl to be just as street smart as she is and never let a man think she needs him for anything. This twenty-one-year-old, four-foot-eleven-inch diva has a figure to die for and men of all shapes, sizes, and ethnicities are always trying to get close enough to her to get that number. She's smart enough to use her looks to get almost whatever she wants from a man, but money and trinkets are not what she longs for. She wants true love.

"Mama, I'm home," Kalitha said as she unlocked the apartment door and walked inside, accompanied by her younger cousin Lavonda. "You here?"

"Hey, Aunt Tina," Lavonda said. "You got something in here to eat? I'm hungry."

Lavonda is always hungry, or at least that's how Kalitha described her. They are three years apart and daughters of two sisters, but Lavonda's mother made sure she didn't just go to school, she excelled scholastically. She pushed her hard because she wanted her to escape the hood one day. This is Lavonda's senior year in high school and, finally, she's able to stay out till midnight and hang with her cousin. Hanging is just what she does as often as she can. These days, wherever you see Kalitha, you're most definitely going to see little Lavonda close by.

"Girl, get your head out of that refrigerator," Kalitha remarked as she tossed her bag on the couch and plopped down on a chair at the kitchen table. "You've been spending too much time around Wanda, and her greedy butt done rubbed off on you."

"What you talking about?" Lavonda asked.

"You know what I'm talking about. You come right in the house, barely say two words, don't even shut the front door, and just run straight to the fridge. Who does that?"

"'Cause, after all that crazy mess that went down at church today, I'm hungry!'"

"You always hungry, girl."

"Whatever. Seriously, why you come grabbing me and pulling me all out into the parking lot, trying to see if the police caught Pastor Weldon or not? You said you didn't care nothing 'bout what happens to him, so why you had us looking around all over the place, tryin' to find out where he's hiding?"

"Lavonda, I don't care 'bout that man. I'm just tryin' to make sure he don't be out somewhere hiding in my spots. I don't need five-o snooping around where I keeps mine."

Kalitha and Lavonda were sitting at the table, talking and didn't even realize that Tina had entered from her bedroom. They were so busy texting on their phones and digging through the kitchen cabinets that they had no idea she had heard most of their conversation. Tina came in, eating a ham and cheese sandwich, smacking on some Lay's potato chips and drinking a Bud Light. She sat down on the couch to see if there was a good movie coming on TV.

"What foolish stuff y'all talking about?" Tina asked abruptly. "What you mean about five-o snoopin' around here? I told you, Kalitha, don't bring no mess up into my house. Now Lavonda, if you're hungry, you better get them crackers or pecans out that cabinet you've got your head stuck in and fill up on that, 'cause I done ate up all the ham."

"Dang, Auntie," Lavonda replied. "You need to get some food in this place."

"You want somethin' to eat, you better start bringing some

groceries up in here!" Tina responded. "This ain't the Eighth Street Mission. We don't just give away food over here."

"Mama," Kalitha interrupted, "I thought you was gonna go see Terrell today. You know he be wanting one of us to come down there and see about him."

"Girl, your brother don't want nothin' but for somebody to put money on his books," Tina remarked. "If I'd known he was gonna end up being this much trouble when he got older I would have never agreed to raise his little bad behind when your uncle left him here." Terrell was really Kalitha's first cousin, but they'd been raised like brother and sister since she was about a year old. Tina's brother was a heroine addict and had dropped his son off one day at her doorstep when he was just a baby.

"But Mama ..."

"Don't 'but Mama' me! He don't do nothin' but gamble it away and get into fights down there. I told that public defender to stop calling me; I can't help him."

"Ooh dang, Aunt Tina! I'm lovin' those shoes you're wearing. They are hot. You should have let me wear them to church this morning."

Lavonda had totally disregarded what Kalitha and her mother were talking about because it was a conversation that always ended the same way. Kalitha loved her brother, sure enough, but he wasn't ever going to change and Tina had almost lost what little money she had trying to keep him out of trouble and bailing him out time and time again.

"You like these shoes, huh?" Tina replied. "Well, just like them from over there 'cause you ain't fittin' to wear these, girl. One of my mens bought these for me, honey, and I makes sure they keep me stylin' *all* the time! They know the deal. If they wants to sample the meat, they've got to put somethin' on these feet."

Tina and Lavonda burst out laughing, slapping each other a high five. The two of them acted more like sisters than aunt and niece. One was trying to be older than she was and the other was trying to reclaim a youth that had long passed.

"Yeah, I like that," Lavonda stated to Tina. "That's good, but what about this: If they wants to feel it poppin', they first gotta take a girl shoppin'!"

Kalitha looked at both of them like they were straight crazy, but she knew they were far from finished.

"You're learning, baby girl," Tina replied. "But try this one right here: Oh, I can sho' make a brotha scream and holler, but first I'ma need to see that dollar!"

"Yeah, Auntie, that's good!" Lavonda said, laughing loudly. "I used this one last week on this knucklehead: Once I get to workin' it, you'll be crooning like a singer, but won't be no playing on this good stuff, till I gets a bling-bling on my finger!"

Taking all that she could, Kalitha yelled out, "Hello! I was talking about Terrell, my brother! Can we *please* get back to that? Oh my God … both of y'all just so nasty!"

"Whatever," Tina said. "You better listen, baby girl, and let me teach you how to handle these men. They are all weak and only want one thing from you. So you need to wise up and learn the game, or you're gonna end up being the one getting played."

"Yeah, Mom, you've told me that all my life, but I'm looking for the right one. The one who's going to treat me like the queen I am and the one who's going to love me for me, not for what he can get from me."

"Well," Lavonda said, "just call me when you find the one that can buy some groceries!"

"Kalitha," Tina continued, "I don't know how many times I've told you that love is overrated and a big lie anyway. Don't nobody love you for you; they love you until they get what they want from you. Once they get what they want, they dump you so they can go find the next piece of love to love."

The doorbell rang and Tina motioned for Kalitha to see who was at the door. Kalitha wasn't done talking to her mother, but she proceeded to answer the bell as it rang for the second time. She unlocked the door without even looking through the peephole to see who was standing there because her focus was still on the conversation with her mother.

"Overrated?" she pushed back, frustrated. "So what, I'm just stuck in this life, chasing a dream that will never happen? I'll just end up being somebody's baby mama and live off the government the rest of my life? That's your life, Mama, not mine. I want more than that. You should want me to have more than that!"

The two of them continued arguing, neither budging from her position. Vickie stood outside the door in the hallway, listening to all the commotion, and since no one was opening the door, she opened it and walked on in. "Little girl," Vickie said to Kalitha, "I can hear you all the way out here, and whatever you're whining about, can you put it on hold for a minute? I need to talk to your mama, child.

Vickie Washington—or "Cinnamon" as most people know her—was raised in a Denver suburb, but has made the ATL her home for the past seven years. She met Tina shortly after moving to the South, and though their initial encounter was rocky, they've become the type of friends who keep it one hundred all the time. She's been dating Officer Raylon Jackson off and on for the last three years. She earns her living as a dancer and bartender in one of the upscale gentlemen clubs on the north side of town. She grew up fast but managed to put herself into college for three years, until she was nearly raped

JAMES E. CHANDLER, SR.

by a respected professor one night while coming out of the library. He was someone she trusted, and the trauma of it all abruptly changed her life and her attitude about a lot of things. Tina's been good for her self-esteem, and she's become close to Kalitha and Lavonda alike.

"Vickie," Tina said, "girl, bring your fat behind in here, and I hope you got my money I loaned you last week. You know this ain't no credit union over here and I needs mine."

"There you go. I ain't even got in the house good and the first thing out your mouth is, 'Where is my money?' Why don't you ask me how I'm doing or if I had a good day or not. Why don't you ask me how's my mama doing down at the nursing home?"

"Well, one, I can see how you're doing. Two, I don't care about how your day's been; and three, you already know I ain't never liked your mama no way, girl. So don't stand there acting crazy. Sit your tail down and answer my question. Do you have my money?"

Most of the time, Tina was funny and a lot of fun to be with. She could find humor in just about anything, but she did not play when it came to her money. Nobody had given her anything. She has amassed what she has because of her shrewd business tactics. She counts every nickel and squeezes blood out of every dime. So when she put her beer down on the coffee table, sat up, reached into her purse for a cigarette, and pulled off her earrings, it was crystal clear that she meant exactly what she'd said.

"Dawg, girl," Vickie exclaimed. "You act like it was a whole bunch of money or something!" Vickie reached into her purse and pulled out her wallet. She grabbed several bills and flipped them through her fingers, counting down the stack. "Here, trick. Here's that sorry five dollars I borrowed from you. Dang, sometimes you get on my nerves!"

"You're lucky I didn't get up on your head, girl. I don't care how much it is; I've got to have mine. I told y'all I ain't got time to be playin' with you little girls who say you got good men but still be broke all the time. That don't make no sense."

"Vickie," Lavonda cut in, "speaking about your man; did you know Raylon came up in our church this morning, trying to arrest Pastor Weldon?"

Kalitha grabbed her juice, got up from the kitchen table, and sat down on the couch next to Tina. "Yeah, Cinnamon," Kalitha said, "I'm glad you're over here 'cause I need you to get your raggedy boyfriend cop on the phone so I can speak to him. I need to talk to him about something."

"I told you don't be calling me by my stage name unless you're gonna be droppin' a twenty in my string. I talked to my baby earlier, and he told me he was locking up the preacher man from y'all's grandmama's church. Said something about he killed a girl downtown on Fifth Avenue."

"Yeah," Kalitha confirmed, "that's what we hear, but I don't know about that. I've been around him this past week and, though I know he's dealing with some fools uptown, he just don't strike me as no murderer."

"I know he's not," Lavonda declared. "I've been trying to tell all y'all that Pastor has just been up under a lot of stress since his divorce. It's not easy being a pastor as some folk think it is. I mean, I don't know what he deals with every day, but I know those folk at the church can be crazy. I mean it got crunk up in there today!"

"What do you mean 'it got crunk up in there today'?" Vickie asked.

"Cinnamon, girl," Tina chimed in, "child, everybody's talking about it. They said your boyfriend dropped in on the rev. at the church today with a warrant, but the preacher broke out running. It's been all over the news that five-o's out looking for him. Where you been?"

"Girl, you know I work all night. I don't be up looking at no news, especially on Sunday morning. I be getting my sleep on."

"Vickie," Kalitha said, "that's why I need to talk to Raylon. I got a call about an hour ago, and I think they've got the wrong dude."

"Kalitha, what are you talking about?" Lavonda said, sitting up. "You haven't said anything to me about that."

While they were talking, Tina took another sip of beer and a drag on her cigarette. She had been leaning back on the sofa with her feet up on the coffee table, but then she slid toward the front of the couch and said to Kalitha, "Looka here, girl. Just leave that mess alone and mind your business. This ain't got nothin' to do with you and whatever mess that preacher got himself into. Let him and his God get him out of it. Your sorry daddy's in jail, your brother's in jail, and the last thing I'm gonna let happen is for those crooked cops to link you up with this mess and put *you* in jail!"

"You're straight talking crazy!" Vickie exclaimed. "Raylon ain't no crook and he's not out there putting anybody and everybody in jail just because! Anyway, I thought you grew up in that church. I remember a few years ago some young, good-looking preacher was over there, but I think he got shot right in front of the church. Isn't that right?"

"Hey, I heard that's what that lady evangelist was telling Portia's mom earlier today," Lavonda said. "I think she was married to him or something."

"You're talking about Linda," Tina stated. "Linda Bell. We grew up together. She's from around here."

"I don't know anything about that," Kalitha continued. "But I know that I need to speak to Raylon about this thing. Something's not right. Something's just not right!"

Just then Vickie's phone rang. She took it out of her purse and realized it was Raylon calling. Before she answered it, she looked at Kalitha. "Girl, you must be psychic or something 'cause you just spoke him up."

"Hey, bae," she said while putting her Bluetooth to her ear. "We were just talking about you."

Raylon Jackson also grew up out here in the hood and he knows most of the city's offenders personally. He should. He ran with them as a boy and then arrested a large number of them as a sixteen-year veteran of the force. He's got enough experience to be a homicide detective or work as a special investigator, but this kid from the streets would rather stay connected to those streets. He's seen and done a lot since joining APD and has made a few dedicated friends in high places, but he has also acquired more dangerous enemies than his colleagues.

Raylon's been married and divorced three times, and though he hasn't had success in any past long-term relationships, things between him and Cinnamon seem to be working out better than anyone expected. They live together on the east side of town and both work long hours, so maybe their regular absences make the heart grow fonder, indeed.

"We who?" Raylon inquired. "What you mean y'all been talking 'bout me?"

"I'm at Tina's," Vickie said. "Your name came up 'cause Kalitha said she needed to talk to you about what happened at their church this morning. What's that all about?"

"You said Kalitha's there? Yeah, put her on the phone. I definitely need to talk to her right now!"

Chapter 3: Holding On

"And Joseph's master took him, and put him into the prison, a place where the king's prisoners were bound: and he was there in the prison" (Genesis 39:20).

OKAY, WE'VE TALKED ABOUT EVERYONE ELSE AND WHAT THEY'D been dealing with today, so let me tell you about what I'd been dealing with. Man, it was hard to keep up with all of the sounds you hear coming from every direction in the jail. Earlier tonight, I heard a bunch of water steadily spilling to the floor from somebody's overflowing toilet. Instead of the jokers in the cell working together to fix the problem, all they wanted to do was fuss and cuss about which one of them was going to clean it up.

Then down the hall I had to listen to these self-acclaimed street-rapping gangbangers beat on metal bars and make up the most God-awful rap songs I've ever heard in my life. You've got about fifteen to twenty knuckleheads thumping and clapping to conflicting rhythms, each trying to outdo the other and prove how poetically powerful he is. The saddest part is that the rest of us had no choice but to listen because we were all part of a captive audience in there.

The worst, however, was this irritating phone that continuously rang, and rang, and rang. The noise came from the back hall area, where the guards hang out, but for some reason nobody made a move to answer it. Apparently, they were either too busy or just didn't give a you know what.

Well, there's no need to keep complaining about the accommodations and acoustics in there because that's just the way it is in an overcrowded, underfunded, foul-smelling city jail. So let me finish telling you what happened when the good Reverend Doctor Charles David Weldon, III arrived to this wonderful facility of ours.

I've known the captain that runs this joint longer than I should have. He's hard and tough, but fair, and he did not appreciate the unnecessary commotion that was coming from the walls of his jail earlier this evening. The guards are well disciplined, the security's extremely tight, and the prisoners understand that their time in lockup is not going to be met with many pleasantries at all. Most hope their day to be heard is coming sooner rather than later because doing even a week there feels more like being in state prison.

I got there around three o'clock this afternoon, but this dude Anthony had been there a good, long while. He is either very stupid or he just wanted to get caught, from what some of the other fellas told me. I mean, who walks into a liquor store and holds it up with a styling brush and comb anyway? Tomorrow is going to mark his one-year anniversary inside and, still, he hasn't been given a date as to when he's going before the judge for sentencing. He'd been scheduled to give his version of that night's events before, but something always came up that postponed his day in court. So tonight, he did what he'd been doing since day one: reading scripture and singing a self-composed melody he swore God gave him in his dreams.

"'A fire devoureth before them,'" he read softly from Joel 2:3. "'And behind them a flame burneth; the land is as the Garden of Eden before them, and behind them a desolate wilderness; yea, and nothing shall escape them.'" He continued, this time talking to God. "Nothing shall escape them, huh? Yeah, that's what I feel. Seems like no matter what, I can't escape, but why? Can you just tell me that? I did what you told me to do. I got them to the hill. I showed them where it all went down. You gave them a chance to change, but what about me? Why don't I get another chance?"

One of the corrections officers told me that you could literally set your clock by Anthony. The same time every night, when the sun began to go down, he began coming up. He walked back and forth in that six-by-twelve cell, wearing the county-issued orange and black jumpsuit with the Bible cupped tightly in his hand. He never holds conversations long with any of the other men, but he could talk to his Lord and Savior all night long. The guards grew tired of threatening him and telling him to be quiet because he was not going to quit his ritualistic evening cadence until he completed each phase.

"I mean I know I did wrong and I know I shouldn't have stormed out angry, but I was young ... I was foolish," he continued. "You know that, Lord! I just don't think it was fair that somebody like him was able to keep going, but the bullet hit me ... and it was over; it was just over. You brought me back to help him, but she doesn't know me ... She doesn't recognize me. You won't even let me tell her I'm sorry! Then you say wait? I've got to just wait? I'm trying with every bone in my body. God, you know I'm trying! But when—when will it change for me? How long must I wait?"

He spoke in manners that were often difficult to understand, as if he'd existed in a time before the present, and it did no good to ask what he meant because he would just break out into a song. Did he sing one tonight, you ask? Of course he did ...

"I wonder when what was spoken over me will come to pass ... will come at last," he began singing. "And I wonder where I will be when You're there to reveal unto me what You promised me. But I'll wait until my change comes. I will wait, wait till my change comes. Lord, I'll wait, wait for my change ... I'm going to wait for the promise, wait for the promise. I'm going to wait for the promise, wait for the promise. I wonder now if I'll make it somehow to that place You prepared, that I know You're there. And I wonder what will become of my dreams. Can I hold on until my promise is real? So I'll wait until my change comes. I will wait, wait till my change comes. Lord, I'll wait, wait for my change ... I'm going to wait for the promise, wait for the promise. I'm going to wait for the promise, wait for the promise."

This went on for almost three hours, and then finally, just as abruptly as he had begun, he stopped. He stood up from a kneeling position, placed his Bible back on the window ledge, pulled off his jumpsuit, and lay down silently on the bottom bunk. He closed his eyes and was getting ready to go to sleep. I would have let him sleep too, but since he'd kept me up, I decided to keep him up.

"Finally!" I told him. "Dude, I didn't know when you was gonna stop whining and singing over there. Jesus Christ! All you did for the last three hours was complain, cry, fuss, and yowl like a wounded cow on his way to the slaughter house! What kind of foolishness is that? You's in jail, son! Suck it up. Be a man. Stop all that girly whimpering and stuff. Shoot, you done woke me up out of my good sleep!"

"I'm sorry," he said. "I didn't mean to wake you up. I'm just waiting on someone. He'll be here shortly. I'll keep it down. I do apologize."

"It's too late to apologize and say I'm sorry now. You done already woke me up, boy. I can't go back to sleep after I been all interrupted from my beauty rest. You gonna talk to me now, and make it interesting too. God, I hopes you ain't boring, talkin' like that preacher of mine was this morning."

Then this clown had the nerve to ask me if I was really in church this morning.

"Hell yeah, I was in church this mornin'! What you tryin' to say, boy? You saying I don't go to church? You saying I'm a heathen, or sumthin' like that? You tryin' to punk me, or somethin' like that here? You got somethin' you wanna say to me, huh? You tryin' to insinuate somethin'? Huh? I don't play, boy! I ain't the one! I'll whoop yo' black—"

"No, sir! No, I'm not saying anything at all like that. You just caught me off guard a little bit when you said something about your minister this morning and—"

"Minister? Partna, I didn't say anything about a minister, boy. I said preacher! What are you, a Lutheran? Apostolic? Wait a minute ... you one of those Jehovah Witnesses, or something? Lawd, I hope you're not one of them, 'cause y'all be gettin' on my nerves with all that doubletalk stuff. Oooh God, I sho hope you ain't one of them, but that's better than being one of those boys handing out those God-awful pinto bean dip pies on the corner. You ain't one of them are you? That's why you said minister? You follow that Minister Farrakhan fellow?"

"No, sir, I'm not Muslim or Jehovah Witness. I'm a Christian. I just said minister because you said preacher. Anyway, I apologize for getting it wrong. What church do you attend, if you don't mind my asking?"

"No, I don't mind you asking nuthin'. It don't mean I'm going to tell you, but I don't mind you asking. I'll tell you where I go to church. I attend the Auburn Avenue Missionary Baptist Church, but don't ask me who the preacher is 'cause it don't matter. All you need to know is who the very fine chairman of the deacon board is. That's what you need to ask me."

"Well, who is the very fine chairman of the deacon board?"

"Boy, you slow. You just so slow. *I'm* the chairman of the board, which means I am the H.N.I.C! Oh yeah, you want something done in this church or in this city, for that fact, you've got to deal with me. You've got to talk to Deacon Willie A.P. Lester, Jr. Watch out now!"

I had to burst out laughing right there, but not too hard because I was still buzzing from the liquid nourishment I'd had earlier. Shoot, truth be told, I almost fell back down on the floor. Okay, now you've probably guessed why I got locked up today. I like to drink. So what, sue me. Is it my fault that the police don't have anything to do on Sundays but pull me over just because I chose to drive on the wrong side of the road? I didn't hit nobody or nothing, but they didn't care about that.

So there I was, back in the hot seat again, but there was a problem that I'm going to speak to the mayor about. You see, normally when I come down there they just let me sleep it off in the nice area upstairs. They gave me some lame excuse that because it was so crowded today I was going to have to spend the night in the lower level with the *real* criminals. I didn't like it but what could I do? My plans were to just get in there and sleep till morning, but some fool decided to put me two cells down from this Anthony fellow.

"Well, Deacon Lester," Anthony said, "it's my pleasure to meet you, sir. I'm Anthony. Maybe I can attend your church one day and hear your pastor preach."

"Son, you can come to my church anytime, but you ain't gonna wanna hear my preacher. Humph, I don't be wanting to hear him. For some reason, a bunch of them foolish women down there wants to hear that mess he calls preaching."

"Oh, so I take it that he's not your type of preacher, huh? What's his name?"

"His name? Oh really? Well let me say it to you like he be sayin' it on Sunday mornings. He gets up, with his phony self, and says, 'My name is, the Reverend Doctor Charles David Weldon, III.' He thinks somebody cares about his name, but I know I don't care at all who the Reverend Doctor Charles David Weldon, III is. I don't care one bit!"

Suddenly, while we were talking about that preacher, the main door opened and in walked Officer Raylon Jackson. I couldn't see him but I recognized his voice right away. He was talking trash like always, and I thought he was alone until I heard it. Yep, I would recognize that bootleg preacher's voice anywhere. The man Raylon was marching into my area was none other than the good Reverend Doctor Charles David Weldon, III.

Before I could catch myself, I hollered out, "What in the devil is that hypocrite doing in here?"

"Hey, pimpy preacher," Raylon said to Weldon. "Sounds like somebody in here knows you already. You gonna fit in real good up in here tonight."

I don't suppose the preacher even knew at that time that I was in there. We hardly talked at church, and though I knew too much about his business, he didn't know anything about mine. He started doing the same thing that all the new ones do when they first come inside; he started begging.

"Listen, Officer Jackson," Weldon replied, "I told you that I don't belong here. I didn't have anything to do with what happened to that young lady! You *need* to believe me!"

"I don't *need* to do anything right now, Rev., but lock your little butt up in this cell. I've got to give it to you though," he said while putting him inside the cell between Anthony and me, "you got some skills. You had me chasing you all over the place, and the way you dipped into that building and out the back was a smooth move. Yeah, I'll give you that. But like I keep tellin' y'all, I may not get you right away, but you best believe I'm gonna get you sooner or later."

"Officer, I don't mean to be disrespectful and I know you have a job to do, but I'm just trying to get you to understand that you have the wrong man. I'm not that man who would hurt an innocent young woman in any way."

"So who did it, Rev.? I mean we found your prints all over the place. We know she called your cell twice that night. We have two witnesses who say they saw you go in the room with her. We may not have found the gun yet, but it's just a matter of time before my boys find out where you dumped it. Oh, you're that man, Rev. Yeah, you're that man."

Weldon's never been in trouble before, and he was visibly shaken and nervous. I almost felt bad for him ... then I thought ... *nah*. I thought he was gonna wet his pants when he heard the cell slam shut behind him. His eyes were watery and his head stayed down the whole time he was being ushered inside. He never looked up to realize that I was in the next cell.

Raylon removed his handcuffs from his wrists through the bars and was turning to head back upstairs, when the door opened again, but this time it was Saundra walking in, carrying a briefcase and wagging her finger in the air.

"Raylon, that's enough," she said with a stern tone. "Pastor Weldon, don't say another word to him! I can't believe you brought him down here, knowing good and well that I was on my way to represent my client. You probably haven't even read him his rights, and by the time I finish with you and the assistant district attorney, you'll both be looking to make new career moves!"

This is the friend of Kim that I said I would tell you about later. Saundra Williams is a divorced criminal attorney, who knows her way around a courtroom. She defends her clients as if she is fighting for her own life. She was born and raised in Southern California and was taught that lawyers were needed to help defend good people who couldn't fight for themselves. She moved to Atlanta several years ago and connected with one of the most powerful and prestigious African American firms in the country. She has become very good friends with Kim and agreed to represent Weldon as a favor to her.

"Hey, hot chocolate," Raylon casually replied. "You missed me, didn't you? I know y'all were having some good booty-shakin' church this morning. But like I told you, I had a warrant for your boy here, and as you already know, Big Pappa Raylon always gets his man."

"Raylon, what you've *got* is probably contagious, so you need to make an appointment with your doctor and see if he can remove that fungus growing up out of your neck! Now move out of my way so I can talk to my client!"

I tried, but I just couldn't hold my peace any longer. It was time for me to let this preacher man know that I was there. "I knew it! I knew it! I knew it! Y'all wouldn't listen to me when I tried to tell you, but I knew it! I knew this gangster wasn't no real preacher; I just knew it!"

"Lester?" Weldon said. "Deacon Lester, is that you? What are you doing in here?"

"Yeah, preacher man, it's me! It's capital L.E.S.T.E.R. in the flesh! I don't believe it. I can't believe that of all the places I could have been to avoid seeing you, I've got to see you up here in my joint. Lawd have mercy!"

"Check this out," Raylon cut in. "Y'all know each other? Lester, you know Reverend Super-Freak, here?"

"Watch it, Raylon!" Saundra commanded.

"My bad, sweet and low. Just having a little fun with yo' boy, here."

"Deacon Lester is the chairman of deacons at my church," Weldon said. "I have a strong idea why he's here."

"Stop right there, now!" I yelled. "It *ain't* your church! You just in here for a season, but looks like your time's about up! You should have never been voted in anyway. My brother was more qualified than you. You probably paid off them fools on the committee. They're just weak and triflin'!"

"I told you, preacher man," Anthony quietly said. "You can run, but you can't hide, preacher man."

All five of us were now in this one conversation together, so we just had to jump in with our comments at the first opening.

"Raylon," Saundra said. "I demand you let my client out of this cell right now! It's apparent that you have some sort of conspiracy going on here to intimidate Pastor Weldon! How dare you put my client in a cell between two obvious repeat offenders, who are intent on harassing and inflaming him? You get him out of there right now!"

"Anthony?" Weldon inquired. "What's going on here? This is no coincidence and no accident. I saw you the night that girl was killed, and I know you know the truth! I don't know what game you're playing or what all this means, but I *need* you to start talking and telling me now. Just what in the—"

"Hey, that's enough noise out of you, preacher!" Raylon interrupted. "It's lights out and I've got to get upstairs and fill out all this paperwork. All three of you just shut up! Come on, girl, I've got to get up out of here now. Come on!"

"Raylon, get your hands off of me!" Saundra protested. "I'm not going anywhere without Pastor Weldon. Now unlock that cell and get him out of there!"

"I'm not unlocking anything, and you are coming with me or you'll be the next one spending the night in a cell."

She pushed back hard and made demands in her most lawyerly tone. She did a good job too, but Raylon had the power of the badge, and all he had to do was key up the radio for help, and she would have been spending the night in a six-by-twelve for women.

She finally complied—reluctantly—but she complied. Raylon escorted her to the door, opened it, and out they went.

Chapter 4: Sold Out

"And he shall send his angels with a great sound of a trumpet, and they shall gather together his elect from the four winds, from one end of heaven to the other" (St. Matthew 24:31).

It had become eerily quiet and very dark in the lower level of the jailhouse. It had been almost an hour since Raylon and Saundra had left, and within minutes the entire area had gone silent. Anthony, Pastor Weldon, and I were sitting on our bunks, reflecting and wondering what more would become of this night and if joy was actually coming in the morning.

Though Anthony was two cells down on my right, I could see his shadow on the floor in front of me as the moonlight and yard lights came through the windows. He was sitting almost motionlessly on his bed, looking up toward the ceiling. I could tell that he held a blank stare, as if he was intently watching and waiting for something or someone to move.

Weldon was right next to me, so I looked around the wall and saw that his head was cupped between the palms of his hands. I could tell that his soul was broken as he surely replayed the events of the day. How could a day that began with shouts of praise and thanksgiving end with nothing but groans of sorrow? Well, since there wasn't much I could do to help either one of them, I decided that I might as well just go ahead and help myself. Don't tell nobody but I had snuck a little something-something inside, and I'd been waiting on it to get real quiet so I could do what I do. I reached under the bottom left corner of my mattress and pulled out a small bottle of Hennessy that was going to do me a world of good.

You probably don't know this about me, but I'm a singer, if I say so myself. Oh yeah, I put it down during devotion on Sunday mornings; we just need to find some real musicians who can flow with me when I start charging the atmosphere. I mention that because I was minding my own business, enjoying a little sip of my black cognac and convincing the whole cell block that I should be the next contestant on *The Voice*, when out of nowhere that clown Anthony interrupted my song. Man, I was crooning and laying it down like Luther when he burst out with his crap.

"Excuse me, Deacon, can I talk to you for a minute?"

"Say man, what you bothering me for? I was just about to get to that special chorus, and you interrupted me!"

"I'm sorry, but earlier your preacher suggested that he knows why you're down here in lockup, but you never said why they arrested you."

Weldon decided to lift his big head from the palms of his hands and interject his two cents into this conversation that I didn't want to be apart of in the first place. "Really?" Weldon chimed in. "You can't smell—I mean you can't *tell* why Willie's in here? Man, you can get high from the fumes coming from over there."

"Oh, wait a minute, Little Richard," I told him. "I know you not trying to call me out! I wouldn't have to get *drunk* every Sunday morning if your no-preaching self knew how to do more than just bore us to tears week after week!"

"Willie, your problem's not with me; your problem is with yourself! I've done nothing but try to be decent and fair with you. I treat you no different than anyone else, and all I ever get from you and your cronies are complaints and criticisms!"

"There wouldn't be nuthin' to complain about if you'd just

leave and go on back to that psych ward they got you from!"

"Hey brother," Anthony said to me, "aren't you being a little hard on the preacher? I mean I know he's made some mistakes and all, but I think this time he's really ready to make a change."

Now this dialogue was flipping back and forth in every direction. We were all standing up and looking at each other through the bars in our cells. I was just about to get Anthony straight when you know who had jumped in the way again. When he'd heard Anthony questioning me, he decided that he would take advantage of the opportunity to interrogate him.

"Wait a minute, partner," Weldon said. "It's time we get to the bottom of some things. Who are you? I mean who are you really? I went to Leona's diner and you were there. When I was coming out of the hotel later that evening, I saw you following me. Then when I ended up on that hill, I looked up, and you were there! Man, I even see you lately in my dreams! Who are you? *What* are you?"

"See, there you go!" I said to Weldon. "You always poppin' off at the mouth with a bunch of questions, like somebody owes you something. That man ain't got to tell you nuthin' 'cause you don't need to know nuthin'! I left church early today, but I heard that you had the police down there looking for your black tail! What's that about? Why don't you answer *that* question, Rev.? Come on, preacher man, you ain't got nuthin' to say now, do ya? What's up, preacher man? Cat caught your tongue?"

"Willie, step off of me. I'm not talking to you right now. I'm trying to find out how this man seems to know so much about me when I don't know anything about him. So come on now, fella," he said while looking at Anthony. "What's your story? Just what is it about you, partner? You seem to know something about me, but I don't know anything about you!"

"You want to know something about me?" Anthony said. "Well, all right, preacher man ... Maybe it's time you learn the truth about everything. Here it goes ..."

Just as Anthony was about to inform Weldon of what he knew, the main entry door swung open and Big Wanda walked in. That chick was switching her big behind from side to side and talking loud like only she can. She came in here, waving and blowing kisses like she was the main attraction atop the Disney float in the Macy's Day Parade.

"Hey, everybody! she said. "Heeeeyyyy! Big Wanda's in the house! Close your mouth and stop drooling. I know you ain't seen nuthin' this fine and this good in *forever!* You don't have to pinch yourself, baby; you're not dreaming. This is real! *All* this is real!"

She came walking down the corridor, calling these brothers out by their names, which lets you know right there she's been around the block one too many times. She walked past Anthony and stopped right in front of Weldon's cell.

I found out when they were booking me that this is the chick who's been trying to get to Weldon for a while now. They say she joined the church this morning after I had left and that she'd brought all of her bills from the house with her to church in hopes that this fool Weldon would pay them. I was looking at her like she'd lost her mind, but she wasn't paying me any attention at all. The only thing she was looking at right then was Weldon. She was in there in a hot pink sweater, some black leggings that were way too tight, and flip-flops that exposed the biggest crusty feet I've ever seen on a woman in my life. She was clearly very happy to see Weldon, but he was less than enthusiastic about seeing her. Oh yeah, and back to those feet. She didn't need a pedicurist; she needed a welder.

"Hey, sugar," she said to Weldon. "So they finally got you, huh? Bless your heart. Well don't worry, baby, 'cause Wanda's here to ease your troubled mind. You may not know this yet, but I joined your church right after you left this morning. Oh, yes I sure did, and the first thing I signed up for was the prison ministry team. You see, I figured you were going to be in here sooner or later."

I couldn't help it. I knew she wasn't talking to me, but when you come into my neighborhood, I'm gonna find out what you doing there. So I poked my head out between the bars, smoked her over pretty good, then said, "Weldon, is this one of your women? Well at least your taste has improved some."

That joker acted like he didn't hear me. Instead of responding to me, he talked to her like I hadn't said a word.

"Excuse me, Wanda, is it? I only have one question to ask you: How in the world did you get in here?"

"Oh, baby," she responded, winking and smiling. "Half of your congregation is upstairs clowning and acting a straight fool up in the lobby. While they were raising sand, I just walked in the side door, acted like I was going to the bathroom, and came on down here. Now I know you a little detained at the moment, but see, my gas bill's a little behind and they talking about cutting it off, so I figured I'd see if you can help me out. You know, raise me an offering?"

That was my opening. You know I had to say something. "Did I say your taste has improved? My bad; I spoke too soon. This girl right here ain't nothing but a mess. A hot mess!" I cracked myself up right there. I started laughing so hard that I almost fell on the floor and bumped my head. I guess she didn't find it amusing at all, because she flipped around and looked at me like I was the baby's daddy who ain't paid child support in fifteen years.

"Oh, hold on, grandpa," she said to me. "Are you talking about me? Am I hearing right? You're laughing at me? 'Cause what's coming out of that cage smells like a mixture of Old Spice and cheap vodka! You ain't got no room to be talkin' about anybody, with your drunk, tired self!"

Now I might have been a little tipsy. Okay, I was drunk—whatever. But what you *not* gonna do is try to clown on me without me handling my business. I said to myself, *If she wanna go there, then we going all the way there!* I had to get this chick straight!

"Oh yeah, sweetie, I've been drinking since early this morning. Po-po got me for a DUI when I was leaving the church. So that's why I smell the way I do. Now I've told you my reason. Why don't you tell us why you smelling like a soiled baby's diaper and looking like Flavor Flav!"

"Oh, no you didn't!" she yelled. "You calling me ugly? 'Cause you so ugly, the last time you went into a haunted house, you came out with an application!"

"Oh yeah, young lady? Well you so ugly, your doctor is a vet!"

"That may be, old man, but you so ugly, on Halloween, your mama made you do trick or treat by phone!"

"Well, sista, you so ugly, the valet took one look at your mug and told you to park in the handicap spot!"

"You so ugly, baldhead, that your grandfather took you to see the monkeys at the zoo, but when the zookeeper saw you, he shook his hand and said, 'Thanks for bringing him back!'"

Wanda and I were going at it good until the preacher butted in.

"Really? I mean really! I've got to sit up in here listening to all this? God, I can't believe I'm in here! What have I done to deserve this? God, please take this whole nightmare away and let me start all over again! Please!"

"You know what, preacher man," Anthony said, "that's the best thing you can do. For too long, you've tried to handle things your way, and each time, you fell further and further down."

"He fell down," I said, "because that Jackleg is low-down! Y'all don't know the truth about this man, but I do!"

"Deacon Lester," Anthony said to me, "your older brother wasn't ready for the assignment to lead the church, but Pastor Weldon was."

"Man, what are you talking about? You don't know my brother! You don't even know me. Who are you, and how you gonna be talking about my family?"

I didn't appreciate Anthony, once again, putting his nose into grown folks' business. Talking about he knows me and my family. He don't know anything about me!

Wanda jumped in and said to me, "I hope he knows somebody who can point you in the direction of the shower!"

"I *do* know your brother," Anthony continued. "And I know you as well. As a matter of fact, I know all of you better than you might know yourselves."

Right then the lights flickered on and off and a strange smell suddenly crept into the area. It started freaking me out a little bit, and I didn't know what was going on. I wasn't by myself; everybody felt this.

"Okay, this is getting very strange," Wanda said, backing up. "I don't know what kind of weird stuff y'all got going on down here. And anyway, I've grown a little tired of y'all company. So why don't I just let you boys have your male-bonding moment. I'm going back upstairs to see if the rest of them have been arrested yet. Bye now!"

Wanda left the same way she'd come in, just swearing in her mind that she was the finest thing on two legs.

"Okay, she's gone," Weldon said. "Now let's get back to the question at hand before anyone else comes down and interrupts us. Once again," he said to Anthony, "and for the last time, my brother ... who are you?"

"Willie," Anthony said to me, "I knew your brother and I knew him well. I knew him because he was my deacon a long time ago."

I've been around, and I've seen a lot in my day. I made it through two tours in Vietnam and beat a heroine addiction shortly after getting back stateside. I've seen crazy and I've done crazy, but this Anthony dude was a different kind of weird. I just couldn't put my finger on it. I didn't know how to respond. I just listened to what he said next to Weldon.

"Pastor," he said, "you know the beautiful woman of God that serves as your associate minister ..."

"Linda?" Weldon cut in. "You talking about Evangelist Linda Bell? What does she have to do with this? How do you know Linda?"

"Well, today I'm a messenger of the Lord. He sent me to you. The Father sent me to *all* of you. Last Saturday, when I brought you to that hill, I wanted you to see that God was giving you another chance. He's giving you a chance to change."

I had to jump in. "Hey, man!" I said. "You said you know my brother, but that's impossible. My brother died years ago. What are you talking about?"

"I knew him because I was once his pastor," Anthony said. "I was married to Linda. We had a terrible argument one day, and I left the house in anger. I drove to the church to do some work and blow off some steam, but as I pulled up, I ran into some activity going down in front of the church. A fight broke out between two rival gangs, and when I stepped in to try and defuse it, I was shot. Yeah, I was shot that night. I died that night."

"Hold on a minute!" Weldon declared. "This doesn't make any sense. What are you talking about you were shot and died that night? Man, have you lost your mind? You must be crazy!"

"No, preacher, it's true. I left too soon because, like you, I wouldn't listen to those people that God had placed in my life. You were in danger, but the Father gave you a chance to make it right. He gave me the same opportunity, but I didn't take it. Today, Linda wouldn't even recognize me, and I miss her so much. Anyway, my time's almost up. I'm just here to tell you that it's time you surrender your all to our God."

I couldn't take it anymore. I was bitterly blowing a gasket, and this joker had gone too far! Nobody understood the depth of respect and admiration I had for Pastor Bell. That man had helped me through some of the toughest times in my life. When I returned from Vietnam, Bell was the only one who saw something special in me. I saw things over there that no one should have to see. I saw the worst in men and I was done dealing with all men, period. That's until I met Pastor Bell. That was my pastor, and I loved him.

"Wait a minute," I said. "You're telling me that you are—or you were—Pastor Bell? That's beyond crazy. That's ... insane! That's impossible! Man, I loved that man! He saved my life! As soon as I get out of here, it's me and you, fella! You are *not* going to be playin' them games and disrespecting a true Man of God, who showed me the way."

"Willie, you started drinking when you lost Sheila and your baby girl. They died together in that accident, coming to pick you up from the airport, and you've been blaming yourself ever since. It's not your fault though."

I don't know how he knew that about me, but he did. The only man that would have known that about me was Pastor Bell.

"Listen, things are about to change for both of you," he continued, "but it's time you start working with one another and not against each other. God has a plan for your life, and you're only here so He can get your attention. It's your time, guys. Don't waste it. Don't let it pass you by."

"My God!" Weldon said, stunned. "But how? I mean when? I'm still struggling to wrap my mind around what you've just said, but I do know one thing: there is a purpose for my life. Everything must change. Everything changes today."

All of a sudden there was a loud explosion outside. Whatever it was, it rocked the walls of the jail and set off the alarms. The power went out and it got pitch black in there for a few seconds. Everybody was freaking out until the emergency backup lights came on. The guards started running down the hall with their weapons drawn. I guess they were trying to find out where the commotion was coming from. It got crazy in there and all of us were trippin' more than a little bit. All of us, that is, except for Anthony.

Chapter 5: Let My People Go

"And the Lord spake unto Moses, Go unto Pharaoh, and say unto him, Thus saith the Lord, Let my people go, that they may serve me"
(Exodus 8:1).

I WAS TOLD LATER THAT THE SCENE UPSTAIRS IN THE MAIN LOBBY was no better than what was transpiring in the other areas of the jail. Nobody seemed to know what was going on or even where the explosive noise had come from. The captain was at his desk behind the counter, trying to restore order after the explosion and power failure. There were officers still trying to book prisoners who were already there when the chaos had broken out. There were also citizens upstairs, fussing and complaining about what was going on and who was going to ensure the safety of their incarcerated family members. I understand it was a madhouse.

"Hey, get control of that prisoner and get him downstairs right now!" the captain yelled at one of the policemen in the lobby. "The rest of you, sit down and be quiet or you'll be spending the night in the cage. Officer," he bellowed at one of the rookies working the intake desk, "get on that phone and tell SWAT I want some men in full riot gear and on the east wall in two minutes! What are you waiting on? Get your butt in gear. Don't just stand there looking stupid! I swear befo' God!" he shouted while banging his fist on the desk. "Just when I'm ready to clock out and get out of here, this crap happens!"

"Hey Cap.," Raylon said as he burst into the room, "what's going on up here?"

Saundra was right on Raylon's tail, no more than fifteen feet behind him, as he ran into the room. The two of them had just made it up the back staircase after barely making it out of the elevator that had stopped when the power went out. She was still very upset at Raylon for dragging her out of lockup and away from her client.

"Raylon, get back here!" Saundra demanded. "How are you going to just drag and push me away from my client like that? You get back down there and get Pastor Weldon up here right now!"

"Girl, will you be quiet! Don't you see we've got something going on here? The last thing I'm worried about right now is Kim's sugar daddy!"

"Officer Jackson," the captain interrupted. "We've got a breach! I need you to secure the outer lobby area."

"Excuse me!" Saundra said, addressing Raylon's superior. "Are you the one in charge here? My client has been detained unjustifiably, and this academy reject is not doing anything to resolve the matter. I need you to stop whatever it is you're doing and get my client out of that cell!"

I heard that the captain looked up toward Saundra, slightly lowered the eyeglasses on the bridge of his nose, and took a deep breath to try to calm himself before responding to her demands. "Lady, are you for real? Does it look like I give a flip about what you want? The jail's on lockdown till I know what's going on here. Now, Officer Jackson, like I just said, get to that front door and make sure nobody gets in and nobody gets out!"

"Yes, sir! I'm about to shut it down right now."

Raylon moved Saundra out of his way and darted for the main doors. She was still waving her finger and fussing, but he paid her no attention. Just as Raylon reached his hands out to secure and lock the doors, they swung open. He was met by

Mary, Linda, Leona, Martha, Portia, Sharon, Elaine, Kim, and, of course, Q.T.

"Honey," Mary exclaimed as she pushed her way into the room, "I don't care who you trying to keep in, but I can sure tell you who you're not keeping out! Now move out my way 'cause I know you not in charge of nuthin'!"

Raylon was doing his best to keep the church members from just barging their way inside, but it didn't work. They came in strong, ready to do whatever it took to get their beloved pastor out of jail.

"What in the world?" Raylon fussed back. "Oh, absolutely not! I'm not havin' it! Now listen here, Mama Klump, take Buddy Love and all the other Klumpetts and back that thang right on back up outta here! We have an emergency situation going on and this is *not* the time nor the place for yo' little prayer meeting, or healing and deliverance service, or whatever you call yourself doing."

"Raylon, where is Pastor Weldon?" Leona inquired. "You all better *not* have done anything to him! He told you this morning that he didn't have anything to do with hurting that girl!"

"That's right!" Portia yelled out. "We came to get our pastor out of this jail tonight, and we are *not* leaving without him! Do you understand that?"

Kim walked over to the counter where Saundra was still engaging the captain. She got her attention and began talking to her. "Saundra," she said, "they told me you were here. Have you seen Charles? Have you talked to Pastor yet? What do we need to do? I can't believe this is even happening!"

"He's downstairs in a cell, where he should not be! I was just about to get him out when we heard some loud noise, and then this fool, here, ran me out."

"Officer Jackson," the captain said, "who are these people? Get them quiet and secure that door!" He was still trying to manage the madness that had broken out on his watch, when he realized how disruptive the members of the church were becoming in the lobby. "Now, I need all of you to sit down somewhere and shut up!" he yelled at everyone. "We don't have time for this right now."

"Well, you better make some time, Kojack, and change that tone in your voice!" Sharon shot back. "'Cause apparently you don't realize who I am. I am the president of the Auburn Avenue Missionary Baptist Church choir!"

"Girl," Q.T. interrupted, "what kind of crazy pill have you been taking? How you gonna be talking to that man like that? Excuse me, Officer," Q.T. said, "this one is confused. She didn't take her medicine today and—"

"Q.T., shut up and get out of my way!" Sharon interjected. "Don't you see me talking? Now where was I? Oh yeah. Listen, I've been up all day, dealing with trifling, envious, folk who don't understand the level of my anointing and imperativeness of my singing; and what I'm *not* going to do tonight is put up with rude behavior and loud talking from some—"

"Sharon, for once I agree with Quincy," Linda quickly said before she could finish her ranting. "Please sit down somewhere and be quiet and let me get some information."

Linda walked over to the desk and began engaging the captain in a more calm and respectful tone. As she tried to ascertain some information about Pastor Weldon, Q.T. and Sharon continued to bicker with one another.

"Excuse me, Officer McClendon is it?" Linda started, reading the name on his badge. "We believe you have our pastor, Pastor Charles Weldon, somewhere in your facility, and you must know that he is not guilty of what you all are charging him with."

"Um, reverend lady," Raylon interjected, "I believe I told you earlier today that I had a warrant for y'all's preacher man, and I don't care what you think he hasn't done. My paperwork says he's our man and he's not going anywhere tonight."

"Wait a minute, Raylon," Mary jumped in. "You're about a good two seconds from me turning you over my knee, son. Now, you done got a little bit beside yourself and must have forgotten that this one here is my baby sister and I'll hurt somebody about mine!"

"Everyone, please calm down!" Elaine said, trying to bring some order to this tense evening. "Let's start again because all of this bickering is not getting us anywhere. There is a way to do everything, and this is not helping at all!"

"I'm still not so sure he's innocent," Martha chimed in. "I mean think about it: if he didn't do anything wrong, then tell me why he ran and didn't just turn himself in?"

"Turn himself in?" Portia protested. "Listen, I know how these police work, and once you've been accused of anything, you're guilty of everything. My brother's always been mistreated by these so-called officers of the law. They are not to be trusted at all."

"Elaine," Leona said with an aggravated tone, "I know your daughter here loves the pastor, but she's got just too much mouth on her, and you need to get more control of your children. When I was coming up, children were seen and not heard."

"Hey, old lady," Portia responded. "I don't hardly see you in church! Why are you down here anyway?"

Kim had become very frustrated with all the back and forth still going on at the jail, just like it had been a little while ago at the church. She was not getting the response she needed from anyone in position of authority and all this unnecessary, unrelated conversation was working her nerves. "I don't have time for this nonsense," Kim shouted. "I came here to get my m—" She stopped quickly, realizing what she'd almost said. She looked around, hoping nobody was paying close enough attention. "I mean," she continued, "I came here to get the pastor out of jail and all of you are just wasting time instead of getting something done!"

"Ooooowheeee! I knew it! I knew it!" Kalitha suddenly said while standing up and shaking her neck.

The members of the church had rushed in so quickly and started in on Raylon and the captain that they hadn't realized who was already seated in the lobby. Tina, Lavonda, Vickie, and Kalitha had all been sitting in the back, just watching the church folk act a straight fool. They had all just seen and spoken to one another in the women's lounge of the church this morning.

"Kim," Kalitha continued, "in the bathroom this morning, you said, 'For the last time, I am not sleeping with Pastor Weldon *anymore*!' I guess what you said, in a sense, was right, 'cause it sounds like to me whatever you and the good rev. been doing does not involve *sleeping* at all."

The four of them burst out laughing at the look on Kim's face as she realized her secret was clearly no longer kept.

"Lord Jesus," Mary said, looking around at everybody. "I should have just stayed in the alley today, 'cause them folk out there seem to have more sense about themselves than some of y'all up in here today!"

"Kalitha," Saundra said, stepping in to defend her girlfriend, "I told you earlier that what you are *not* going to do is try to put my girl in the middle of some atrocious, dalliance fantasy that you've conjured up in your little mind."

Tina's laughter came to an abrupt halt when she saw and heard the way Saundra was speaking to her daughter. She hadn't been at church this morning, but Kalitha had informed her on the ride over of what had gone on in the lavatory this morning. She stood up and started walking slowly toward Saundra with her hands on her hips and a lot of attitude on her face.

"Oh, I know I'm going to jail tonight!" Tina said. "Who do you think you're talking to? Now, I don't understand what you just said, but, chick, it didn't sound good. I'm 'bout to pull all dem cavities out yo' mouth for talkin' to my baby like that! I don't care how many po-po here. They all know me anyway!"

"OK, I just wanna know one thing before the fight starts," Lavonda said to the captain. "Do y'all got somethin' back there in the kitchen to eat? You know, like some chicken wings, fries, some ice cream, or somethin' like that?"

It wasn't until Tina made her move toward Saundra that Raylon realized his woman, Cinnamon, was in the room. "Vickie," Raylon said, "what you doing down here with these criminals, bae? You supposed to be heading down to The Cheetah to make Big Daddy some money!"

"I know, baby. That's where I was headed, but I had to stop by Tina's on the way, and when I got there they were talking about some preacher you locked up today. By the way, why were you whispering earlier on the phone when I talked to you? You sounded like you were stressing out about something, but then you asked to talk to Kalitha. What was that about?"

"Cinnamon, I didn't call you tonight. I've been down here dealing with this bootleg preacher and some drunk deacon from your girl's church. When I put Weldon inside there was this other dude already in the cell next to his. Call you? No, baby, it wasn't me."

"Lawd Jesus! Lawd Jesus!" Leona declared with hands lifted in the air. "Would you just look at what these things got on up in here tonight. I have never seen more filth and trash up in one place in my life!"

"I have," Q.T. said, laughing. "In your diner! I swear the health department needs to shut that place down 'cause you even killin' the rats out in the alley."

"Q.T., shut up and go find you a boy toy downstairs to play with," Sharon proclaimed. "You just always saying something stupid at the wrong time."

"I'm just going downstairs to find Pastor myself," Kim cut in. "You people are doing nothing but wasting my time and working my nerves."

Everybody seemed determined to keep up as much rumpus and ruckus as they possibly could. Tina had said her piece and was working her way back to her seat, when Kim called her name to direct her next comments at her.

"Let me explain something to you, trick!" she said. "Please understand that you were not the only one raised in these streets. I can handle mine when I have to and don't let your mouth deposit a check that your butt can't cash!"

Tina snatched off her wig and threw it to the floor. She flipped around super quick and kicked off her shoes. She had no plans to come down there to deal with anybody, but tonight somebody stood in need of an old-fashioned, country ass whoopin'. "Well don't stand there talkin' about it!" Tina insisted. "Get over here and be about it! I ain't whipped nobody's tail since this mornin', and it looks like your attitude needs some correcting!"

"Okay," Q.T. said, "I'm about to go back to the house 'cause ain't nobody gonna be getting no blood all on my new shirt. I've got to be at the midnight musical tonight and I can't be going up in there with no diseases and mess all over me and stuff."

The two ladies charged toward each other, determined to finish this debate with the laying on of hands. Just before they connected, several church members stepped between them and stopped it before they were both arrested."

Changing the subject and putting the focus back on the reason why they were there, Martha said, "Did anybody do a background check on Pastor Weldon? I mean I know he can preach and sing, but is that all you looked at before you brought him to the church? Did anyone bother to see if he had a past?"

"We *all* have a past," Linda responded. "We all have done things we're ashamed of. God knows I have. We have all fallen short of God's glory, but He's given us another chance to correct our wrongs, and we just have to calm down, people, and let God guide us in the right direction."

"Linda's right," Elaine interjected. "Look at us. Look at how we're acting. Calling one another names and standing in the middle of a police station about to fight. This is not right! I love my pastor and I want him out too, but nothing *right* can come from all this *wrong!*"

"But Mama, what are we going to do?" Portia asked.

"We're going to stop everything we're doing right now and call on God to heal us and help us. He's a God of peace and a God of love. He, and He alone has the answer."

The power suddenly came back up and the main lights flickered back on. Everyone was still very agitated, but as Elaine tried to bring peace, it seemed to be returning to the atmosphere. Elaine turned and walked over to the captain. He was looking down at several reports that had just come in. She tapped him on the shoulder. He looked up for a second then went back to what he was doing as if she weren't standing there.

The tear that was forming in her eye immediately dissipated and this time she thumped him on his shoulder and said, "Sir, I demand to see my pastor right now!"

Chapter 6: It is Well

"And we know that all things work together for good to them that love God, to them who are the called according to his purpose" (Romans 8:28).

IT HAD BEEN A CRAZY DAY TO SAY THE LEAST, AND I WISH I COULD tell you the madness was over, but it was not. I could hear everything that was going on upstairs in the lobby through a vent in my cell, and combining that with what the guard had already told me, I figured there was still more to come in this seemingly unending, ridiculous night. These members had lost their minds, and I could hear it all, including who was making the biggest fools of themselves. I had decided, however, that I didn't want to be bothered anymore with their issues; rather, I wanted to find out just what the preacher man was doing in the hotel with that girl—whoever she was. There were still a lot of unanswered questions that he needed to address, and what better time than right then. So I stuffed some tissue inside the vent, took a couple of swigs of my Hennessy, and started banging on the wall till I got his attention. He asked me what I wanted and told me to just leave him alone. He claimed he didn't want to talk about anything and that he was praying and conversing with God, but you already know I wasn't trying to hear that.

"Preacher man, don't even try to pull that crap on me. You're gonna open your mouth and we're going to have a good Q and A session here tonight. Every Sunday, I have to sit up in the front row of the church and listen to you lie and smooth talk these stupid members, who think your stuff don't stink. I sit there listening to you go on and on about some deep revelation and interpretation you've received from the Lord in your time of meditation, but we both know that's a lie. Yeah, you're good at wanting folk to hear you squall and tune up behind that book board, but now that you're on the other end and I'm looking for some answers, you act like you don't want to say anything?

You think you're the only one who knows the Bible, and the rest of us are just a bunch of backward, country ignoramuses, who cling to every word that comes out of your mouth. Hell, I remember the first day you came to the church and I said to myself then that you were the most arrogant, condescending, playboy preacher that I've ever known. I guess you thought that a fancy car and a tailor-made suit would convince all of us that you were the best thing that's ever happened to this church, but dog, you were sadly mistaken. Yeah, you're right, I didn't like you and, yes again, my brother was the best choice for Auburn Avenue, but I was outnumbered by those you'd already brainwashed."

"Willie, what are you talking about? I didn't brainwash anybody. Just leave me alone."

"Oh, so you don't wanna talk now, huh?"

"Just leave me alone, Deacon. I don't have anything to say to you."

"You don't have nothing to say? Is that right? The almighty, all knowing, all wonderful, all powerful Dr. Charles David Weldon, III doesn't have anything to say? Really? The man who's always telling the rest of us what we need to do and how we need to live? The man who's got degrees from this school and that school and who boasts of the books he's written and the awards he's received? That man all of a sudden doesn't have a topic of debate or discussion of which he can elaborate and interject an opinion of supreme intellectual insight and wisdom? Well, why don't we start on something simple? Why don't we parley on the subject of this girl you killed?"

I know I hit a nerve right then because it sounded like old boy punched the wall as hard as he could while slinging some good old curse words my way. I had that joker on maximum hot and he probably wanted to bring his tail into my cell and try to whoop up on this old man's head. I heard Anthony trying to chime in with his two cents and interrupt what was about to go down, but I didn't allow that. No, this was the moment that I'd been waiting on for a long time. The guards were still way down on the other end of the block, dealing with whatever that loud noise was and I was determined to push the good rev. until he popped one way or the other. It may not have been right, and I'm sure that the alcohol aided in my antics, but really, at the time, I just didn't care.

"Willie, I told you that I didn't kill anybody and I'm tired of hearing it from you and everyone else who doesn't know what they're talking about! I've had all that I can take tonight and I'm sick and tired of people like you weighing me down with your boneheaded accusations. What is your problem with me? What did I ever do to you? I know you've had it out for me since day one and all you've done since I've been at that church is give me grief about everything. I created programs to raise money to help pay off the church, and you turned around and accused me of scamming the people out of their savings for my own personal greed. I spent years building up the big brothers ministry to help boys who were growing up without a father, and you turned around and started a rumor that I was some sort of pedophile, preying on little kids. I put together the praise team and personally worked with the singers to record our first church album, and you turned around and tried to convince people that I'm gay because I can play the piano, sing, and direct the choir.

I am a Man of God but I'm also a divorced man, and I reserve the right to enjoy the companionship of a young lady when I so choose. I don't have to answer to you or anybody else, for that matter, on who I spend time with away from the church. But I will tell you that I met someone very nice, who was extremely smart and beautiful. Someone who I had a lot in common with and who understood the calling on my life and the needs of my heart. I found someone who ended up meaning a lot to me and who was brutally taken from me just when I needed her most. Yes, I was meeting up with her at the hotel that night. And yes, I was planning to make love to her that night. And yes, I know it was wrong in the sight of God and I was going to be chastised for it, but I loved her. You didn't even ask me how I felt; you don't even care how I felt when I walked in that room and discovered that some demon had taken her from me. All you did is jump on the bandwagon and assume right away that since I'm a preacher who was about to commit fornication, I must also be a preacher who would commit murder. It makes me sick just thinking that the chairman of the deacons in my church would actually accuse me of doing something that heinous to anyone."

I have to admit that I began feeling a little bad for what I could tell Weldon was feeling and what he was going through. Deep inside I felt he probably didn't hurt the young lady, but I just wasn't going to give him the satisfaction of knowing that. There was a lot going on in my life right now and some of the things that this fellow Anthony had said earlier were still troubling me big time. I wanted more answers from Weldon, but I was also tripping about the things this other cat had revealed. I mean he was talking about my former pastor, Rev. Bell like he was actually him, and he even had knowledge about how my wife and daughter were killed a long time ago. I needed to understand that too, but Weldon and I still had so much unfinished business that I was determined to address tonight.

I told him, "Look, preacher, I don't know what you did or what you didn't do to that girl, but it must be more than what you're letting on. The guards told me that the investigators have some strong evidence against you and that you were seen walking away from that hotel. Look, I get that you wanted, as you say it, some companionship. I understand that completely because, like you, I'm alone too. I remember when your wife left you and I know that was rough, but it was nowhere near as hard as what I went through when God took my wife, Sheila, and my daughter from me. They were all I had in this world, and once again, the woman and baby I loved were taken from me. I say once again because though she was my first wife, she was actually the second woman I'd loved.

You see, preacher, a long time ago, before you came to this church, I met and fell in love with an incredible woman. She was a preacher too, but back then the Baptist church didn't give preaching licenses to the women who had a calling on their lives. She could only evangelize in the holiness and apostolic churches because they were more advanced and accepting of female preachers back then. I was young and in the military back then. We were in love and talked about getting married, but Uncle Sam shipped me off to Vietnam before we had a chance to tie the knot. I was thousands of miles away while my woman was out here going from city to city, telling people about the goodness of the Lord. Crazy thing is, one night when she was coming northbound on I-85, some trucker ran her off the road and I lost her. Just that quick, she was gone—or I thought she was."

I realized I was doing all the talking again and this part of the night was not meant for me to go on and on, but I wanted to see what else the good rev. had to say. I was getting ready to probe deeper, until I was strangely interrupted by the things Anthony began to say.

"Pastor Weldon," he whispered. "Pastor Weldon, you're right. You don't owe anyone here any answers, but you do have to answer to your Father. You see I know so much about you because I was sent here for you and I was sent here to you. Everything that's happened has been by divine design and it's all meant to get your attention. You, sir, have an amazing gift and calling on your life. I'm not talking about the manner in which you deliver the Word on Sunday morning or the skill you've developed in teaching and motivating others, but I'm talking about the depth of sincerity in your heart. Like David, you're a man after God's own heart and He loves you more than you know. Before you were born and before your parents conceived you, God had a plan for your life and a purpose for your service. He protected you from so many traps the enemy had set and each time you survived the onslaught, instead of humbling yourself and bringing your flesh under subjection, you chose to move on to the next opportunity to evoke your will above His.

Remember when the prophet Isaiah came to Hezekiah and told him to set his house in order or he would surely die? Or remember when Gabriel showed up and told Zechariah that he and Elizabeth were going to have a son, even in their old age? Well, Hezekiah believed and obeyed the prophet and God extended his life, but Zechariah rejected the validity of Gabriel's salutation and this cost him the ability to speak for nine months. Your life has been spared, but the plague of disobedience fell on someone that you dearly loved. Sometimes the sins of others affect our lives in ways that are very unfair, but then sometimes our sins infect the future of others in ways that are irreparable. I know you're innocent of this crime, but you were about to commit one of equal shame, and He just would not allow it."

Now I was sitting on the edge of my bed with my mouth wide open, floored by the things I was hearing. I'd never seen or heard the voice of an angel, and though I always knew they were around to protect us and watch over us, I just pictured them to be floating or flying heavenly hosts that could only be seen in the spirit, not in the flesh. I know this may sound crazy, but I began sobering up very quickly and filling up with an ocean full of questions that I needed to ask, with answers that I knew would be given. Questions like why did God take my wife and my daughter from me? And why before that did He let my first love be taken away from me? And why did He give me a pastor like Pastor Bell only to replace him a few years later with this Weldon cat?

Just as I was about to speak, there was another loud explosion. The lights flickered and suddenly went completely out. It was pitch black for approximately fifteen seconds, and then just as quickly as the chaos began, it ended. The tissue had come out of the vent and was lying on the floor. The sounds and voices from upstairs returned. The guards started coming back down the corridor. One stopped as he was passing Anthony's cell and yelled out, "Why is this cell door open, and where is Anthony?"

The next thing I heard was the sound of someone hanging up a phone and I heard the captain say, "Officer Jackson, I just hung up with Homicide. Seems like these folk are right. The pastor is innocent. They've got the perp in their office right now, confessing to everything he did. Go downstairs, get him and that drunk, and bring both of them up here so we can release them."

"Now Captain," Raylon replied, "I hear you about the preacher, but why are we letting the deacon out?"

"Because, that one over there, Mary, she paid his bail. She said she knows him."

"Stop questioning your elders," Mary said to Raylon. "Just go get Pastor out of that cell. Now hurry up, fool!"

Everyone began hugging one another as they heard the great news about Pastor Weldon's impending release. Raylon walked out the door and toward the elevator.

"Leona," Martha said, "he may be getting off on this, but there's still a lot of things he's done, and I feel like he should have to explain why he was with that girl in the first place."

Kim looked at Martha. "Oh, he doesn't owe you *any* explanation. Just who do you think you are? It's my understanding that today was your first time even being at the church, and you think the pastor has to discuss his dealings with you?"

"Kim," Elaine jumped in, "you have some nerve! You are part of the reason why good men end up destroying their homes and bringing scandalous mess to the church. Don't you realize how many lives you've ruined? How many people are hurt?"

"Kalitha," Vickie said, "I don't know what type of people you hang with, but if this is the company you been keeping, then, baby girl, you need to find you some new friends. Raylon told me y'all was wild, but y'all worse than the stuff that be comin' up into my club at night."

"Now, Miss New Jersey Turnpike," Mary said to Vickie, "come over here and let me talk to you for a minute."

"New Jersey Turnpike? Why you call me that?"

"'Cause don't you open up your gate real wide and let just anybody drive through once they toss a little change into your receptacle? Now I understand that you be down there at that shake-a-booty house, showin' and doing only God knows what," Mary continued, "but listen, that's not the life or lifestyle God intended you to have. Don't you know Raylon don't really respect you? I mean, how can he respect you when you don't have no respect for yourself?"

"Mary, don't bother this young lady," Linda interrupted. "Don't you recognize her?"

"Don't I recognize her? What you mean? Who is she? You know this girl?"

Just then the lobby door opened and in walked Raylon, followed by Weldon. Everybody ran over to hug and greet him, but Mary pulled Linda over to the side to finish the conversation they were having. The room was buzzing with the sounds of elation and the captain was trying to get everyone's attention.

"Okay, everyone, quiet down please. Once the pastor signs for his belongings and processes out, you can all leave. Then I can finally get out of here and get some rest."

"Thank you, everybody, for being here tonight," Weldon said. "We've got so much to do and so much to talk about, but right now I just want to get out of here and go home!"

"Linda," Mary said to her sister, "girl, you need to finish telling me what you was saying. What you mean asking me if I recognize that stripper over there?"

Linda was about to respond to Mary, but guess who came staggering through the door. Yep, yours truly.

"Daddy?" Vickie cried. "Daddy, what are you doing here?"

Everyone was standing there looking back and forth at Vickie and me with their mouths wide open. They were floored by what they'd just heard.

Vickie broke the silence. "Yes, this is my father," she proclaimed. "Daddy, you were in jail again? What happened?"

"Daddy?" Mary interrupted. "Girl, you know this man? You say Lester's your father? You are his child?"

"Yes, Mary," I said to my long lost first love as I still held on to my liquor bottle. "This is Victoria. She's *our* daughter, Mary."

TO BE CONTINUED ...

ABOUT THE AUTHOR

JAMES E. CHANDLER, SR. is respected for his idiosyncratic style of writing and speaking. He is also an entrepreneur, a recording artist, choir director, songwriter, musician, and playwright. Though he is multi-talented and gifted, he prides himself in being a humble and faithful servant of God.

His message is one that focuses on developing the total person into what God has destined him or her to become, through the love of His only begotten Son Jesus Christ. His purpose is to encourage every man to follow his dreams and maximize his potential.

He is the Founder, Organizer, and Senior Pastor of Marvelous Light Christian Ministries in Lithia Springs, Georgia. What began as a blessed group of 250 people, who were devoted to spiritual growth, became a ministry receiving in membership of more than 2000 souls.

In 1985, he and his high school sweetheart, Kelly Manning, united in holy matrimony, and one year later moved to Atlanta, from Denver, where he enrolled in the Religion & Philosophy program at Morehouse College. Together, they have three beautiful children: Kayla, James II, and Jonathan; and one lovely granddaughter, Lauryn.

He is truly a gift to the Body of Christ and an anointed vessel for such a time as this. On any given Sunday morning you may hear him quoting one of his favorite sayings: "If you look hard enough, you'll see God moving in every situation."

To learn more about James E. Chandler, Sr. and Showitt Entertainment, please visit: www.Showitt.net

Mother
Sis Gray

God Bless! Dedicated
Stay O J
11/1/01

RELATIONSHIPS

your KEY to
Divine Destiny

STACY D. HILLIARD

RELATIONSHIPS
Your Key to Divine Destiny

ISBN: 978-1-943852-61-1 (paperback)
ISBN: 978-1-943852-62-8 (ebook)

Library of Congress Control Number: 2017945082

True Potential
REACH THE WORLD

True Potential, Inc
PO Box 904, Travelers Rest, SC 29690
www.truepotentialmedia.com

Printed in the United States of America.

To all those who have been, (and will be) instruments and examples used of the Lord in fulfilling God's plan and destiny for my life; I treasure my relationship(s) with you